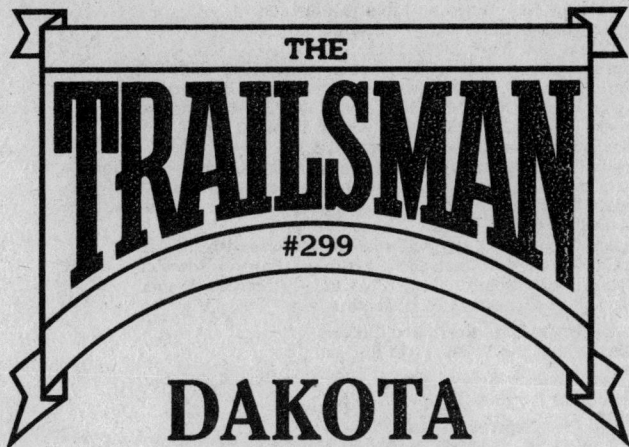

THE TRAILSMAN

#299

DAKOTA DANGER

by

Jon Sharpe

W0013388

A SIGNET BOOK

SIGNET
Published by New American Library, a division of
Penguin Group (USA) Inc., 375 Hudson Street,
New York, New York 10014, USA
Penguin Group (Canada), 90 Eglinton Avenue East, Suite 700, Toronto,
Ontario M4P 2Y3, Canada (a division of Pearson Penguin Canada Inc.)
Penguin Books Ltd., 80 Strand, London WC2R 0RL, England
Penguin Ireland, 25 St. Stephen's Green, Dublin 2,
Ireland (a division of Penguin Books Ltd.)
Penguin Group (Australia), 250 Camberwell Road, Camberwell, Victoria 3124,
Australia (a division of Pearson Australia Group Pty. Ltd.)
Penguin Books India Pvt. Ltd., 11 Community Centre, Panchsheel Park,
New Delhi - 110 017, India
Penguin Group (NZ), cnr Airborne and Rosedale Roads, Albany,
Auckland 1310, New Zealand (a division of Pearson New Zealand Ltd.)
Penguin Books (South Africa) (Pty.) Ltd., 24 Sturdee Avenue,
Rosebank, Johannesburg 2196, South Africa

Penguin Books Ltd., Registered Offices:
80 Strand, London WC2R 0RL, England

First published by Signet, an imprint of New American Library,
a division of Penguin Group (USA) Inc.

First Printing, September 2006
10 9 8 7 6 5 4 3 2 1

The first chapter of this book previously appeared in *Dead Man's Bounty*, the
two hundred ninety-eighth volume in this series.

Copyright © Penguin Group (USA) Inc., 2006
All rights reserved

PUBLISHER'S NOTE
This is a work of fiction. Names, characters, places, and incidents either are the
product of the author's imagination or are used fictitiously, and any resemblance
to actual persons, living or dead, events, or locales is entirely coincidental.

The publisher does not have any control over and does not assume any responsibility for author or third-party Web sites or their content.

The Trailsman

Beginnings . . . they bend the tree and they mark the man. Skye Fargo was born when he was eighteen. Terror was his midwife, vengeance his first cry. Killing spawned Skye Fargo, ruthless, cold-blooded murder. Out of the acrid smoke of gunpowder still hanging in the air, he rose, cried out a promise never forgotten.

The Trailsman they began to call him all across the West: searcher, scout, hunter, the man who could see where others only looked, his skills for hire but not his soul, the man who lived each day to the fullest, yet trailed each tomorrow. Skye Fargo, the Trailsman, the seeker who could take the wildness of a land and the wanting of a woman and make them his own.

Dakota Territory, 1862—
nothing is more dangerous than a man
who has lost his memory. Dangerous to himself—
and to the killers all around him.

1

Traveling through Dakota Territory the day before, Fargo had seen two bandits robbing a stagecoach while a third was busy ripping the clothes off a fetching red-haired young woman who was obviously a terrified passenger.

Fargo was on a hill above the road. Squinting against the blistering sunlight, he could see that the stagecoach driver was sprawled on the ground, probably dead. That would account for the two shots that had caught Fargo's attention.

Another man, probably riding shotgun, stood with his hands up while one of the bandits shot the lock off a strongbox. The lock took three bullets to smash open.

By this point, the woman had been stripped down to her waist, her sumptuous breasts naked in the daylight as she clawed the punk's face and tried to push him off her.

Fargo used his Henry for this particular job. The first target was the rapist's knee. The shot echoed off the twisted line of prehistoric rock that formed a long wall on the far side of the stagecoach.

The rapist cried out and tried to grab his knee, but fell over in pain before his fingers could find the wound.

The next shot smashed the bandit whose gun was pointed at the shotgun rider. His shoulder exploded into flying debris of blood, bone, flesh.

Fargo stood up. "You've had the only chance you're going to get," he shouted, making his way down the small rocky hill. "I want you to put your hands up and then I

1

want the stagecoach man to pick up your guns. You make any kind of move and you're dead."

They dropped their guns in the dirt.

The first thing the shotgun rider did was check on his partner. He knelt down next to the body, but it was clear that his friend was no longer alive.

He raised angry eyes to one of the bandits and then stood up. "He was gonna be fifty years old tomorrow, you son of a bitch."

The rapist obviously hoped that Fargo had been distracted by the bitter words. His hand shot out as he tried to grab the woman again. She had just managed to cover herself with the torn parts of her blouse.

She screamed and lurched away the moment she felt the bandit's hand on her.

Fargo executed the man. He had given clear warning but the man had elected to disregard Fargo's words. The execution came swiftly. The bandit's forehead bloomed with a huge red flower of blood.

Both of the other highwaymen decided that this would be their last chance for freedom. One of them dove for his gun in the road.

He caught a bullet in his temple.

The other man had his gun in his hand by now. He got off two quick shots at Fargo, but he was too scared to fire with any care. The shots went wide. Fargo got him directly in the heart.

Before the echoes of gunfire had quite faded, the shotgun rider walked out from behind the horses and watched as Fargo approached. "Sure glad you showed up, mister. I would've been dead for sure. This is a bad bunch. They've killed two people in the last couple weeks."

The woman came up then.

She was obviously a female of breeding. The white blouse was real silk and the dark blue skirt looked custom-tailored. A thin bracelet on her slender left wrist was gold.

"I'm sure glad you came along, too. He would've killed me after he was done with me. Or maybe all of them would've spent some time with me—and then killed me." She smiled. "I'd shake your hand but then the front of my blouse would fall down and you've both seen enough of me, I'm afraid."

Never enough of *you*, Fargo thought.

"If you'd be so kind," she said to the shotgun rider, "and take the brown leather bag from up top. I've got a couple of blouses in there I could wear."

That had been Fargo's introduction to Amy Fenton.

And what an introduction it had been.

Amy spent the next morning at the bank she'd inherited from her father. She dragged Fargo along to see the town of Tall Rock. He was all shaved up and shiny and she didn't hesitate to show him off as the trophy he was. She was not only the sole female bank president in the Territory, and she didn't bother to hide the fact that as a young woman she still had plenty of appetite for good times and pleasure.

Fargo had been traveling for nearly ten days straight before he met Amy at the robbery scene, so after she was done showing him off and had set about her business, Fargo went up to her vice president, a prim little man named David Culver. He was as stiff as his celluloid collar. His displeasure with Fargo could be read on his face. His expression was that of a man who'd found himself standing in pig feces on a very hot day.

Culver wore a gold cross on his lapel. He clearly wanted everybody to know that he was morally superior to them, and Fargo figured that the small man probably was. Just about everybody, at least as Fargo saw it, was morally superior to Skye Fargo.

"I was wondering if you could direct me to the general store and the gunsmith's shop," Fargo asked pleasantly.

"They're really not very difficult to find," the man said. "The whole business district is three blocks long."

"Well," Fargo said, "I appreciate the information."

The man leaned forward and spoke in a whisper. "You're not the first, you know. She parades you saddle tramps in and out of here like a slave auction."

Fargo smiled. "Interesting you won't tell me where the general store is but you'll tell me about your boss's personal life."

"I'm giving you a warning is all. I just hate to think you'd fall in love or something. I'm just talking man-to-man."

The "man-to-man" remark left Culver wide-open to a nasty crack from Fargo. But Fargo was tough, not mean.

Fargo spent an hour on his errands, and by that time Amy was waiting for him at the office of the Badlands Express, another business she'd inherited from her father. A four-vehicle stagecoach company.

The pride and joy of her fleet was a new-model Concord that was presently the most lavish coach constructed for commercial use. She was excited about showing it to Fargo.

This one was painted bright red. The interior was sleek polished wood with leather-covered benches that could seat eight people comfortably. The horses were already in their traces. Amy had changed clothes. The suit she'd worn had been replaced by a chambray shirt, Levi's and a pair of hand-tooled riding boots. She was somehow even more elegant in these duds than in her more formal ones.

The round-trip she described would take just under two hours, she told Fargo.

Even with all the new types of support mechanisms, a stagecoach ride was still a stagecoach ride, though it was less violent than most of the coaches Fargo had ridden in. At least you didn't get thrown from one side to the other, or crack your head on the ceiling.

Of all the places Fargo had seen on his travels, none compared to the Badlands. Illustrations of prehistoric times were fashionable these days but none could capture the strangeness of the land that rose up on either side of him. Steep cliffs, ragged ravines, rock formations that startled the eye and colors Fargo had never seen before.

Not hard to imagine that giant flying predators had once dominated this land, aeons ago.

Or even that dinosaurs had prowled its spiky crests and twisted rock spires.

"Now I'll be the teacher and you be the student, all right, Skye?"

She wasn't the sort of woman to wait for a man's approval. She plunged right into her lecture about the history of the Badlands, how neither the Indians nor the French had been able to conquer them. To the south of the Badlands was soil so rich, farmers barely needed to plant. Whites and Indians alike prospered there.

But here . . .

Finished with her history lecture, Amy leaned out the coach window and said, "Give the horses a workout, Riley!"

"Yes'm," the driver called down to her. "You just hold on to your bonnet."

She pulled her head back in. "Someday I'm going to wear a bonnet and surprise old Riley." She gave Fargo an impish smile. "In fact, maybe I'll wear a bonnet to bed tonight. I hope you'll be there to see it."

"Fine by me," Fargo said. "As long as that's all you wear."

But there was no more time for flirtatious conversation. Suddenly Riley lost control of the stagecoach and it veered sharply to the right, inching off the narrow rock road.

The screams of the horses were terrible to hear.

Even more terrible was the knowledge that coach and passengers alike were about to plunge into fast-churning water in the deep ravine below.

Fargo hit the top of the door with such force that he blacked out instantly.

2

Water this deep and dangerous was unusual in the area, but there had been a strange cold spell in August followed by the kind of relentless rain that usually came only in spring.

Gullies splashed with water; runoffs could be seen everywhere. The turkey vultures that prowled the vicinity were almost starved out. The rain kept their only food source, the jackrabbit, staying dry and out of sight.

When the pride and joy of her stagecoach fleet hit the water, Amy's first thought was to get the door open and swim to freedom. She was an excellent swimmer and didn't anticipate any real trouble.

She just assumed Fargo could take care of himself.

But in the clear water inside the coach she found Fargo floating facedown. From what she could see, he seemed corpselike. He made no effort to swim. Just hung there. The coach was already half submerged.

Then she saw the streaks of blood mixed with the water. Fargo had been hurt.

Not until now had she felt any panic. She'd collected herself and prepared for the swim to the surface.

But now she'd be responsible for two lives. And Fargo wasn't exactly a frail little man.

She made her way over to him, got her arm under his. She tugged him to the door and then began the process of using her right hand and foot to try to force the door open. She reached through the window and grabbed the handle. With the pressure of the water against it, it wouldn't open. Maybe if she had both hands free . . .

Panic. The water was rising rapidly inside the stagecoach. The surface of the water suddenly seemed as far away as the surface of the moon. No matter how hard she kicked and pushed, the stagecoach door wouldn't open.

She thought of leaving Fargo behind. That was the only sensible way to handle this. It would be so easy, just let go of his arm and concentrate both her hands on pushing the door open. It wouldn't be so bad for him. He wouldn't suffer or struggle. He was already unconscious.

She dropped his arm, confronted the door. Frustration joined panic now as she tried to wrench the handle down. And her guilt was just as bad as her panic.

She couldn't leave Fargo behind.

She turned around and took his arm by the wrist, holding him there while she stretched to reach the door again.

She had just put her hand on the handle when she felt

something thrash violently against the arm holding Fargo. For the next minute or so, she lived out a dime novel.

Here was this powerful man, suddenly awakened and gasping for air. Here was this honorable but trapped damsel in very deep distress. And now the heroics started.

Fargo took her place at the door. At first, he had the same problems she had had. The water pressure against the door made escape impossible. Then he started tearing apart the wood that gave shape to the window.

She'd never seen a man this strong, ripping the lighter wood around the window with such force that it came off in large pieces rather than just slivers.

She was just starting to pass out when she felt his enormous hand grab her wrist and begin to pull her through the opening he'd just created.

Everything moved quickly. Sunlight. Warmth. Fargo laying her out on her back. Tiny rock teeth cutting into her flesh.

"You all right?" Fargo asked.

So many physical sensations, including serious dizziness. But she was collected enough to understand that she was going to be all right. "Yes. I'm fine."

"I'm going back for Riley."

When he hit the water this time, Fargo had recovered himself. Going over into a ravine had turned him into a confused and frenzied animal, but now he knew what he was doing.

The stage was now on its side at the bottom of the water. The horses were still in their traces, drowned.

He swam around but saw no sign of Riley. Sitting up high on the front of the coach, Riley had probably been thrown off at considerable speed and distance.

Fargo had to surface again to draw more breath. He took a long moment to swallow deep gulps of air and enjoy the golden sunlight, and then he returned to the depths of the rushing water.

This time he swam ten yards ahead of the overturned coach. He didn't see Riley's body at first because it was hidden, bobbing behind a jutting piece of jagged rock.

There was nothing he could do for Riley except swim

him up to the sunlight and make sure that he got a decent town burial. By the time Riley was pulled out of the water, Amy was standing up.

When Riley was flat on the ground, she crossed herself and whispered a prayer. She looked at Fargo. "He was a good man. His family's going to be devastated. I'm trying to figure out what went wrong. I wonder if something spooked the horses."

"I've got one more dive to make."

She started to ask him a question but he had already angled himself toward the water. He slipped below easily, and disappeared.

His intention was to find the reins leading from the traces to where Riley had been sitting. He'd been worried that when the stage tipped over it might have made the reins impossible to reach. He started with the dead horses and began following the leather strands back to the stage-coach itself.

He didn't have to go far. At about midpoint, he found where two of the reins had been cut. He worked back to the horses, where he found two other reins in the same condition.

He would have looked further but he'd stayed too long already. Besides, he had the evidence he needed.

He reached the surface moments later.

Once again on dry ground, Skye took his makings out even though he knew the tobacco would be useless. Soaked clean through, of course. He flung them down the rocky slope of the ravine. "Come on," he said.

Amy was still dazed from seeing Riley's corpse.

"Where're we going?" She sounded almost childlike.

"Back to town."

The mildness of the day made walking pleasant. No baking sun. But the problem with the seventy-degree temperature was that it didn't dry their dripping clothes very quickly. And Fargo had one of those drumming headaches that required the serious attention of a whiskey bottle. Whiskey might not banish the headache, but a couple of good-sized gulps would distract him from the worst of its throbs.

For all her femininity, Amy could deal with emergencies

very well. She didn't complain about the walk, the wet clothes, or even how expensive the stagecoach would be to replace. A woman as smart as she was would likely have insurance though, Fargo reasoned.

They walked on, their clothes eventually starting to dry. They looked like bums, their clothes wrinkled, hair plastered all over their heads, both of them stopping every once in a while to take off their boots because the wet leather chafed at their feet—their wet socks not helping any.

"Will we ever know why the stagecoach ran into the ravine like that?" she asked after a mile or so.

"Well, I didn't want to say anything till we got back to town and had a little whiskey and some food in us but—" He could feel her eyes on him. He shook his head. "It wasn't an accident, Amy. Somebody cut the reins. That incident could've happened anywhere. The reins just happened to tear at the worst place possible."

"That's impossible, Skye. Are you sure?"

"Positive. That's why I swam back down there. I wanted to look things over. Now I doubt they meant to kill anybody. But they did mean to do some serious damage to your stagecoach."

"But, Skye, I've never had any enemies like that."

He slid his damp sleeve around her damp neck.

"I'm afraid you do now, Amy."

3

The town looked as prosperous as any Fargo had seen in the past four or five months of traveling. The false fronts were new and clean; the road had been raked well; there were plenty of outhouses so the air smelled reasonably clean; and Amy's bank was two stories of nice red brick. It was the finest building in town.

The afternoon sun lent melancholy shadows to all the buildings; the laughter of the kids just released from the one-room schoolhouse managed to sound melancholy, too.

Nobody had picked them up. Not until they'd reached the town limits had they even seen a horse, let alone a wagon. They were wrinkled, disheveled and very much a curiosity as they moved slowly down the main street, people on the sidewalks eyeing them with great interest.

They just never saw Amy looking like this. That being one thing the jealous women of the town were jealous about—the way, no matter what she wore, Amy always looked perfectly kempt, even if she was in an old work shirt and dungarees and working in her garden. What the hell could've happened to her? And who the hell was the wild man walking next to her? Now there was one son a sensible man would walk wide of. Real wide of.

They stopped when they were one block into the business district.

"Thanks for saving my life, Fargo."

"And thanks for saving mine."

"If you say so. I didn't really do much."

"I didn't really do much, either."

She laughed. "We're just such modest people, aren't we?"

"My middle name is humble."

"How interesting. Mine is modesty." She nodded to her sassy new bank. "I've got my buggy back there. I'm going home to change. Then I'll tell the sheriff about Riley. I'll have the maid prepare a very nice dinner. Why don't you share it with me?"

"Now that'd be right hard to turn down."

The thought of good food almost crowded out the anger he felt. After he'd changed clothes and rested up a bit, he was going to start nosing around. He was determined to find out who'd cut the reins.

"See you tonight then, Skye."

She stood on tiptoe and kissed him on the cheek. Then she went to get her carriage.

4

On the walk back to town, Amy had told Fargo about the livery stable she owned. Her stagecoaches were kept there but its services were also open to the public. She took special pride in having the finest driver in the Territory. Whenever an official came through here, they asked for a man named Yank Channing, a crippled man who'd worked himself up from stable boy in Saint Louis to a driver who excelled at every kind of task, from driving two-in-hand all the way up to driving six-in-hand perfectly matched blacks.

Whenever the governor came through town, he asked for Yank to be his driver.

Yank was shoeing a mare when Fargo came in. "Be with you in a minute," he said.

He was a hunchback with a large head covered with curly dark hair. He had mastered the ability of holding nails between his teeth while he spoke.

He had also mastered the ability of giving somebody a suspicious eye. It was one way of putting every new person he met on the defensive. This trick probably worked pretty well with most folks. But it was wasted on Fargo because Fargo was giving him the suspicious eye, too. Who was in a better position to cut the reins than the man who took care of the horses?

Yank finished with the mare, setting its hoof down. "I'll be right back, mister."

Yank led the horse out the back door of the place. He walked in a jerky, halting way. Any other time Fargo would feel sorry for the hand the little man had been dealt. But not now. Not when the little man was the chief suspect.

"Bet you think I cut them reins," Yank said when he came back, wiping his hands on his leather apron and sticking a corncob pipe in the corner of his mouth.

"Amy come by, did she?"

"Yep. She said not to be afraid of you, that you looked a lot meaner than you really are."

Fargo smiled. "Now there's a compliment if I ever heard one. Did she mention that I also eat little babies?"

"Hey," Yank laughed. "We got somethin' in common. I eat little babies, too." He put out his hand and they shook.

"I didn't cut the reins, Fargo. Got no reason to. This stagecoach line is the best job I've ever had. Pays best, Amy fixed up an apartment for me—and I mean really fixed it up—and the people in this town don't treat me like some freak. Lived in one town where some old ladies and a minister spread the word that I was the son of a witch. I got out of there before they decided to burn me at the stake."

"You make a good case for yourself."

"But just because I ain't the one don't mean I can't help you. You ask me, it was the Indian."

"What Indian?"

Yank took the pipe from his mouth. "Couple nights ago, I was just comin' back from supper over to the café, and I seen an Indian walkin' away from the area where I wash the coaches down. Keep a lot of material in a shed next to it. Including extra reins and things like that."

"You keep it locked?"

"No reason. Nobody ever gave us any trouble."

"You get a good look at the Indian?"

The little man shook his head. "Not really. He walked away fast. Real fast. First thing I did was check everything. Went through the whole shed and then went through the barn here. But I couldn't find anything missing." He frowned. "I never thought of checkin' the reins to see if anybody had played with them."

"Not your fault. Nobody would've thought to do that."

"Thanks for sayin' that, Fargo. Truth is, I feel sort of funny—guilty—about bein' the one responsible. Amy's been so damned good to me."

"She knows you're not responsible, Yank. But tell me more about this Indian."

Yank spat a stream of tobacco juice onto the ground. "Never saw him before. They still don't have much to do with us. Don't trust us. And they've got some pretty good reasons not to." He spat some more tobacco. "Of course, we don't have a whole lot of reasons to trust them, either."

"Nothing special you noticed about him, then?"

"Not really. But he sure acted guilty about something, now that I think back on it. Maybe I should've reported him."

"You did what you could. You checked everything out."

Yank smiled bitterly. "Yeah, except I didn't check the reins."

"Well, if you remember anything about him, let me know, will you?"

"Sure. But shouldn't you talk to the sheriff?"

"Reckon I'll get around to it pretty soon."

Soon came a lot sooner than Skye had figured on.

He'd just left the livery and was headed for dinner with Amy when a burly man with a caveman gait, a sneer and a badge walked right up to Fargo and said, "Hear you'll be eatin' out to Miss Amy's tonight."

13

"Now where'd you hear that?"

"Miss Amy herself. I gave her hell for not reporting that accident to me soon as she got back to town."

"It wasn't any accident."

"That's what she said but when I asked her for proof she said it was underwater." He snorted. "Now that's a hell of a place for evidence to be, isn't it?"

"If you say so."

The dark eyes narrowed. The greasy five o'clock shadow on the lawman's face gleamed in the dusk light. Several townspeople stopped to eavesdrop on the conversation. The sheriff waved them on angrily.

" 'If you say so.' What's that supposed to mean?"

"Well, you could always get a diver to go down there and look at it. He'll find just what I did. Somebody cut the reins so that, sometime soon, they'd snap and the stage-coach would get thrown off the road."

The lawman pawed at his wide jaw. "My name's Ken McLeod." He didn't offer his hand. "I already know your name. And I'm gonna tell you right now, I catch you playin' detective again the way you just did, you're gonna be in trouble. Serious trouble. You understand me?"

Fargo shrugged.

"That supposed to be an answer, Fargo?"

"That's just supposed to say that I understand you. I wouldn't want somebody tryin' to do my job for me, either. But somebody damned near killed Amy and me, and I'd like to find out who it was."

Down the street a player piano thundered into life. As if on cue, saloon girls started laughing loudly. Skye heard the clack of billiard balls, the scraping of poker table chairs being pushed into position and the sighs and nickers of horses hitched to the posts outside the three saloons. When the player piano went into action and the girls who pushed drinks started laughing, that meant it was the official start of night.

"You leave it all to me. I'll handle it all fair and square." McLeod rubbed his considerable belly. His big, busted hands told Fargo that he'd held his own many a time and, being a lawman, probably against great odds.

"You walk easy around here, Fargo."

14

"I just want to find out what happened. Somebody damned near drowned me. And one way or the other, I'm going to find out who that was. You want to do your job, fine. I'll need to be ridin' on from here soon, anyway. But if somebody gives me a lead, I'm going to follow it down."

"Then I'll hear about it—there ain't much goes on in this town that I don't know about—so you'll be doin' just what I told you not to do. And that's when we'll be havin' ourselves a run-in." He glowered. "Why don't you leave it to the professionals? I took some classes on sheriffin', Fargo. I know a whole lot about this job you never will. Now that's sayin' it as nice as I can."

Fargo wondered why the man was being so conciliatory all of a sudden. McLeod obviously enjoyed playing tough; why play otherwise now?

"I'll help you by findin' out the truth, Fargo, and you help me by stayin' away from bein' a detective." Then McLeod said, "If you'd like a beer, be glad to buy you one at one of our fine saloons across the street there."

"Wouldn't want to spoil my meal with Amy."

McLeod winked. "She'd make a mighty fine meal herself, if you know what I mean. I got to admit, she's a true-blue beauty. And with that body of hers— You're a lucky man, Fargo. A very lucky man." Then he said, "And if you stay out of my business, you'll keep on bein' lucky."

5

Fargo could imagine what Amy's mansion would look like during one of the "parties" she told him about during the dinner of roast duck, braised potatoes with cream sauce, cooked carrots gleaming with butter and apple pie.

Seen from a distance, the mansion looked like a fortress, an enormous estate house fashioned from native stone and lined on two sides by looming pines. The barn in back was double-size; the gazebo on the west side was big enough for a band and twenty dancers; and the servants' quarters were in a house that anybody would be proud and happy to live in.

When they finished their meal and their drinks—the wine was as tasty and heady as she'd promised—they went into the parlor, where she showed him paintings of her family from five generations back. Three of those generations had lived in England and, from what Fargo could read into the paintings, had lived damned well. Or else the painter had been ordered to make them look that way.

"Sick of me bragging?" Amy said.

She wore a low-cut silk dress that displayed her sumptuous breasts. A festive green ribbon in her hair matched the dress and set off her green eyes. Her pale flesh was enlivened by faint freckles that added a wistful touch to her femininity. The freckles made it easy to imagine what she'd looked like in her late teens. She'd probably had a long line of young men tripping over their feet and tongues in an effort to court her.

Fargo said, "I thought maybe later we could go down to your bank and count your money."

She laughed. "I had that one coming, didn't I? I'm sorry I went on so long about my family. I got that from my mother. Anybody who ever crossed our threshold got the historical tour I just gave you. I guess I inherited the tendency."

"Actually, it was sort of interesting. That's what this country's all about, I guess. People coming over here from foreign countries and making their mark."

She slid her arm through his as they stood before the gallery of paintings. The push of her breasts against his biceps roused him easily.

"Well, my clan had a little help making their mark. They were rich when they landed here. They just wanted to get away from the king. It seems he wanted to hang them for certain writings that my great-great-grandfather had penned and circulated. It seems he suggested that the king was a lazy oaf, a thief and a coward."

"But other than that the piece was probably flattering, right?"

She squeezed herself to him again. "Are you as much fun in the bedroom as you are in the parlor?"

"Well, I guess there's only one way to find out, don't you think?"

"I think you've probably got something there, Mr. Fargo. In fact, I think we're thinking very similar things."

"That's just what I was waiting to hear." He took her in his arms and kissed her with such fury that she literally went limp in his embrace.

"My God," she said breathlessly, "I may not live through this night."

She got up on her toes and pushed her mouth against his. As he closed his arms around her he could feel her urgency causing her body to tremble. Her lips were sweet, her tongue eager.

He unbuttoned her dress so he could slide his hands over her marvelous breasts. They were large and well rounded,

17

heavy in his hand, just the way he liked them. Abruptly, he slid the dress down around her waist and leaned forward to kiss her breasts, suckle her nipples.

"Ooh, yes . . ." she said, cupping his head and pulling his face against her.

Her skin was so smooth and fragrant that he lost himself in its scent and feel.

"The bed, Skye. Please, let's go to bed."

They walked to the bed and fell on it together. They discarded their clothing quickly and came together urgently. She tripped while stepping out of her clothes and they both laughed, blinding lust making them both sound a little bit crazy.

She fell back on the bed, eagerly grabbing his shaft as he bent to her. "Lordy," she said as she stroked it lovingly. "This should be one of the Seven Wonders of the World."

She smiled at him just before his mouth met hers. But instantly her playful mood vanished and the urgency came up in her again.

And so did his. Everything else was forgotten now that he was in bed with this incredibly beautiful, bright woman.

His tongue found her nipples and as it began to tease them, she started bucking beneath him. But she managed to give pleasure while she received it. She continued to hold his manhood, stroking it gently. She made him shiver when she ran her nails along the underside.

After a time, he started moving down her body. He took his time, the tip of his tongue bringing her to searing new heights of need. Ultimately, his face found her fragrant bush and as he eased himself lower, his tongue working quickly but subtly as he found her womanhood, her cries became frantic. She brought her hips up to meet the pressure of his tongue, and held the back of his head with her hands while he sucked and lapped her into a frenzy, until finally she came with a loud cry. ı . .

He climbed atop her then and slid his rigid staff into her slowly, until he was buried to the hilt. They began moving together then, seeking a tempo that would satisfy both of them, and when they did they went on like that for a long time, enjoying each other until finally neither one of them could hold back.

"Oh, my Lord," she gasped.

Fargo looked down at her and grinned. "My sentiments exactly."

Fargo was near the town limits, headed back to his hotel, when the hidden marksman opened up on him.

Frost on the ground. Half moon. Hoot of owl, chug of distant train. Occasional farmhouse, lighted windows cozy against the night.

And Fargo himself? Sated. She'd been even better than he thought she'd be. He dozed from time to time in the saddle, looking forward to the hotel bed. He'd spent way too many nights under the stars this year. Time for a little bit of good sleeping on a mattress.

And then the shots came.

A damned barrage of them.

Even with his life at stake, he was able to identify the weapon as a Spencer.

As he threw himself from his Ovaro stallion and started rolling on the ground, he was able to see a glint of momentary flame from the timber to his right. He'd been able to count shots, too.

He was pretty sure the assassin would be reloading now.

He decided to surprise the would-be killer.

He threw himself back into the saddle, ducked down, grabbed his Henry from its leather and then charged forward at full speed, cracking the chill night air with enough firepower to totally confuse whoever was shooting at him.

He focused on the exact point in the line of woods where he'd seen the shot flare up. He was at full gallop now, firing down to his last bullet.

Just before he reached the woods, he reined in the stallion, flung himself from the mount and then rushed the dark stretch of timber before him.

Two shots cracked a branch above his head just after he plunged into the pine trees. He ducked but didn't return fire. He needed to establish where the shooter was in relation to that last shot before he wasted bullets.

Two more shots.

The would-be assassin didn't seem to realize that he was making things easy for Fargo to locate him. The shooter

19

was up trail a good twenty, twenty-five feet, no doubt tucked behind some pines.

Fargo wanted to get this over with. There was some spill moonlight on the trail that only made what he was about to do even riskier. But he decided to risk it.

He stepped into a patch of moonlight and said, "Right here!"

Three shots, this time. *Bam bam bam.* One or two of them would certainly have caught him, maybe even killed him, if he hadn't thrown himself to the ground again and rolled under the bullets in order to locate the man with the Spencer.

Fargo, still rolling, took careful aim and hit the man clean in the forehead. There was no doubt he was dead. Nobody survived a wound like that. Fargo didn't get much of a look at the man's death frenzy—the falling backward, the windmilling arms, the knees collapsing, the blood spurting from the hole just above the right eyebrow.

But he heard the crash. The man was so big he sounded like a huge tree that had been felled.

The killing done, the thing now was to find out who the man was. Whoever'd hired him to murder Fargo sure hadn't gotten their money's worth.

6

"Sheriff around?"

The night man was a stubby little fella who'd been reading a magazine when Fargo came in. Must have been a pretty interesting piece because he looked resentful about having to go back to work again.

"Gone home this time of night."

"That's what I figured."

"You're that Fargo."

"I'm that Fargo."

"Anything I can help you with?" He finally forced himself to his feet, though he got a last glance at the magazine as he did so. He wore a black shirt with red suspenders and denims. He had a potbelly that hung over the top of his denims like a large ball.

"There's a dead man slung over the back of my horse."

The night man's hand went automatically to his holster.

"Ease off, Deputy. It was pure self-defense. He was trying to kill me." He looked around the front office. A number of WANTED posters, several yellowing newspaper clippings no doubt attesting to the courage, wisdom and all-around wonderfulness of the current sheriff. A rack of repeaters, an iron stove that was kicking out a moderate amount of heat and an open doorway that led to some cells in the back.

"Can you prove that?"

"Not unless I can get a corpse to talk."

"Then you'd best get him jabberin'. Self-defense ain't worth a hoot unless you got what they call a collaborative witness."

"Corroborative."

"What?"

"You said 'collaborative.' The word's 'corroborative.' "

"Ain't you the smart one."

"I bring him in here?"

"Who?"

Fargo couldn't figure out if this guy could possibly be as dumb as he seemed or was just acting dumb to irritate him. Maybe a little of both.

"I have a dead man slung across my horse. Would you be so kind as to tell me where to take him? Here or direct to the funeral parlor?"

The deputy came around the desk. "You wait here."

"For what?"

"For me to go get a look at the corpse. Then I'll be back."

Fargo shrugged. "I'll wait here."

Fargo went over and helped himself to a tin cup of coffee while the deputy was outside at the hitching rail, looking over the dead man. Fargo hadn't found any kind of papers on the body. Nothing to suggest a name or a place where the man might have come from.

When the deputy came back he had a six-shooter pointed directly at Fargo's heart.

"Put that damned thing away. I already told you I killed him in self-defense."

"Turn around and walk through that door back there."

"I want to see the sheriff."

"You'll see him as soon as I get you locked up."

Fargo knew there was no sense arguing. "I suppose you want my gun?"

"Damned right I do."

"I'm taking it out and putting it on the desk right next to me. I'm not going to give you even half a reason to put a bullet in my back because I think you'd like that too much."

"You're right about that, mister. Now put the gun down."

As jails went, this one was typical. There were four cells back here in the lantern light, and they were identical. Each had two straw mats on the floor for sleeping, a can to piss in and a library's worth of convict wit and wisdom scrawled on the walls—a lot of it about the various things the people who'd stayed here thought the sheriff was.

The deputy got Fargo in the cell, locked in good and tight and said, "Now I'm gonna go get the sheriff."

"I'm going to take a little nap."

"You're right on the verge of bein' charged with murder and you're still gonna sleep?"

"You got any better ideas for entertaining myself?"

The deputy sneered and left.

Fargo hadn't been joking about taking a nap. He was one of those fortunate people who could nap for fifteen minutes or so any time he felt like it.

Which was now.

"You got any idea of who you killed?" asked Sheriff McLeod. They were in the front office of the jail—McLeod, Bosworth, the deputy and Fargo. McLeod had asked his question as if the dead man might be someone important.

Fargo shook his head.

"We don't either," said McLeod.

"Oh."

"You kill a man and that's all you've got to say?"

"I don't have much to say about somebody I didn't know who tried to kill me—except that I'd kill him again in just the same way if I had to."

"Well, that's a nice little statement, Fargo, except for the fact that I don't know that he tried to kill you."

"Not much I can do about that."

McLeod went behind his desk and sat down, leaving Fargo and Bosworth standing.

"Bosworth here thinks I should charge you with murder."

"Well, then I'd do it."

"You would?" McLeod said, his voice revealing his surprise.

"Sure, a great legal mind like Bosworth's—not to mention his investigative skills—I'd do anything he told me to."

"He's bein' sarcastic about me, Sheriff."

"Let me tell you somethin', Fargo. Bosworth isn't as dumb as he looks."

"Nobody could be, Sheriff."

"Is he bein' mean about me again, Sheriff?"

"You'd better watch yourself, Fargo. Bosworth here's my son-in-law."

"I figured it had to be something like that."

McLeod startled Fargo. He brought a meaty fist down on the desk and shouted in full voice, "I'm not gonna sit here and have you mock me. You understand that, you saddle tramp piece of shit?"

Survivors know that there are times to push a man a little further. And there are times when pushing him any further is a form of suicide.

Fargo said, flat-voiced, "I killed him in self-defense, Sheriff. I went out to Amy's house for dinner, just like I told you I was going to. And on the way back, somebody was waiting in the woods for me. I brought in his Spencer. He must've emptied it twice tryin' to kill me. But he wasn't much good when I went into the woods after him. He got confused pretty easy and just kept shootin' at me. I wanted to bring him in alive but he never gave me the chance. I wanted to know why he wanted to kill me—or who hired him to kill me. I'm new to this town. I haven't had any run-ins with anybody. So I was damned curious about why he was shooting at me."

McLeod looked at Bosworth. "Sounds reasonable enough."

"I don't trust him."

"You hungry, Boz?"

"You sendin' me after food again so you can get rid of me?"

"I always pay for your grub, too, don't I?"

"I guess that's true."

The transaction was made. Money changed hands.

"You want anything to eat, Fargo?" McLeod asked.

"Guess not."

"Okay, Boz, guess you can go."

"I still don't believe him. I want you to know that."

"I know that, Boz. I know that."

24

Bosworth left.

"He don't drink. He don't bully people. He don't ask merchants for 'free samples,' and he don't walk around like King Shit. He's not smart, I'll grant you that. But he's a good night man. And he's a good father and a good husband to my daughter, who ain't no prize, believe me. She's even meaner than her mother, rest her soul." He looked right at Fargo. "And you know what?"

"The Pope's gonna make him a saint?"

"I thought we were done with your smart tongue, Fargo."

"All right, Sheriff. Proceed."

"He's got an instinct. Nine times out of ten he can figure out who's guilty and who isn't."

"What happens the tenth time?"

"All lawmen make mistakes."

"Yeah, but when lawmen make mistakes, people get hanged sometimes."

McLeod put his feet on the desk. "What I'm sayin' is that I take his opinion serious."

"Then you think I'm guilty."

"Like I said, nine out of ten. You could be the tenth. I'm of two minds about you and I can't decide what I think about you. So I'll tell you what. You get the hell out of here now and I'll explain to Boz when he comes back. And you stick around town because I'll have more questions for you after the doc takes a look at the body."

"You think I won't run off?"

"You give me your word?"

"I do."

"Then I'm not worried. I take you serious, Fargo. You're a saddle tramp but there's somethin' about you . . ." He shrugged. "Get out of here before Boz makes it back and we all get in a squabble."

Fargo was out the door in six seconds.

7

Silver drops of moisture fell from the branches of the pine trees and some of the paths were muddy. The back and shoulders of Fargo's shirt were wet from last night's rain-drops falling from the trees. The morning itself was sunny, clear and brisk.

Last night's shooter hadn't been very careful. A stampede of bulls would have been more delicate. Foliage was trampled down in several spots. He'd even left a few bullets behind; apparently he'd reloaded so quickly he hadn't taken time to pick up the ammunition that had fallen to the ground.

But the bullets were standard issue. They told Fargo nothing.

After half an hour, he was beginning to think he might have been better off just sleeping in and catching up on his rest.

On his way back to the road, he found the coin. At first Fargo thought he was looking at some strange kind of money. But when he scrubbed the path's mud from the silver-colored piece he realized that it was a promotion tool for a steamboat that worked the river near here, the *Belle Mae*. The thick paper coin entitled the possessor to a free turn at the roulette wheel after he'd paid for his first three tries. Anything to keep the suckers gambling, Fargo thought.

Not long after, he stood in the Western Union office writing out a telegram.

He was in this part of Dakota Territory to see an old trapper named Ham Wilkins, a good friend who'd helped Fargo out of a bad turn with a couple of federal agents several years back. Fargo could have gone to prison for a long time if Ham hadn't been willing to testify for him, something the federal boys hadn't wanted him to do. One of the agents had had a run-in with Fargo a while back and wished most devoutly to see Fargo spend many years getting acquainted with his prison cell and all the terrors that went along with it.

Ham's daughter had wired Fargo that Ham had had two strokes and was dying. Fargo didn't have many friends but those he did have meant a lot to him. He wanted to see the old trapper before he passed over.

His telegram was simple:

ON MY WAY. BE THERE LATE TOMORROW.

—FARGO

Having been up at dawn, when the streets were empty, he was surprised to see all the people and wagons and activities that now flooded the town. It was like an empty stage set suddenly filled up with actors.

He ate a big breakfast at the café and was then on his way back to his hotel when he remembered the steamboat coin he'd found on the trail where he'd killed the assassin last night.

The steamboat office was two blocks away. When he got there, he had to wait fifteen minutes before two long lines of a church group had been taken care of. The women all wore bonnets and were as excited as children. The choir they were in had been invited upriver to sing for a visiting bishop. They were all getting their tickets.

The buxom, middle-aged woman who waited on him looked at the coin and said, "I'll be happy to give you a new one with your ticket."

"I'm afraid I don't want a ticket, ma'am. I'm just trying to find out about this coin."

"Well, it's promotional."

"When did the promotion start?"

She thought a moment.

"Let's see. Last Sunday. Three days ago."

"They weren't distributed before then?"

"No." Then: "Do you mind if I ask you why you want to know about this coin?"

"I'm investigating a murder."

Then she did the damnedest thing. She smiled. A huge, enormous, wall-to-wall smile and said, "I love murders."

"You do?"

"I sure as heck do. Especially the British ones. Every time we go to Saint Louis I buy up a whole batch of them. They have a secondhand store there that always has a big selection."

Fargo smiled.

"I'm glad you're talking about books. For a minute there—"

"Oh, no. Real murders scare me. We don't have many around here, praise the Lord." She smiled impishly. "But I'll be glad to help you any way I can."

She had been so flustered when he'd mentioned murder that she'd forgotten to ask him for any identification, which was fine with Fargo.

"So the earliest anybody could've gotten a coin like this was Sunday?"

"Yes, sir."

"How many boats have landed here since Sunday?"

"One."

"Do you keep passenger lists?"

"As best we can. We don't claim to be a hundred percent accurate."

"You think I could take a look at that one?"

She puckered her lips and thought about it. "Guess I don't see why not. Since you're investigatin' a murder and all."

She reached down under the counter and picked up a long sheet of paper, which indicated that the list would probably be long. But when she handed it to him there were only four names. Three women and a man.

"Light day, huh?"

"Very. But that happens every once in a while. Usually we get twenty, thirty or so. People come to see the Badlands."

Earl Halloway.

"You remember anything about this Earl Halloway?"

"Sorry. Sunday's pot roast day at home. I don't fix up a pot roast and vegetables, the husband and the kids go on the warpath. And we're talkin' eight kids in my brood, so it's quite a warpath."

"You ever steer your passengers to a certain hotel?"

"Oh, sure. The Premiere, down the street. They give each of us five percent of what the bill runs up to. Adds up over a year's time."

"Thanks for all your help," Fargo said.

When he got the door open and was about to step outside into the sweet autumn day, she said, "Hope you catch him. In those British books I read, they always catch him. The only thing I don't like is they never show nobody gettin' hanged. The American ones, they hang people right and left in those books."

Fargo turned to her and smiled. "Seems to be in our nature, doesn't it? We love a hanging."

"Amen to that," the lady laughed. "You can't beat a good hangin'."

8

He didn't sign in as Earl Halloway, he signed in as Earl Brody. He went out one evening dressed in a good suit and a fancy black hat, and came back a whole lot richer from three hours at the poker table. He asked for and received directions to the most expensive brothel in town. He came back from that with a smile on his face as shiny as his new boots. Then he bought a newspaper and went up to his room, and that was the last time anybody had seen him. This was all the night before the night he went and got himself shot. He didn't look like the type to get himself shot but then a fella never could tell, now could he?

"Any chance you still have the things he left in his room?" Fargo asked the walleyed desk clerk who'd been nice enough to supply him with all the rest of the information. After Fargo had pushed some money at him, of course.

"Afraid not."

"You mean he didn't leave anything behind or you don't know what he left behind because nobody's looked yet?"

"Oh, somebody's looked, all right."

"Yeah? And who would that be?"

The desk clerk nodded to somebody over Fargo's shoulder. "That fella right there."

"This man givin' you trouble, Bernard?"

"No, sir. Just askin' a lot of questions is all, Sheriff."

"Probably pretty much the same questions I asked you about two hours ago, right, Bernard?"

Bernard looked nervous. He must have gulped three times in a single minute. He knew he was in some trouble. He just had to figure out how much. Sheriffs just don't seem to appreciate it when you talk to somebody who has no official right to know anything.

"Yes, sir. Pretty much the same questions."

The lawman put a big hand on Fargo's shoulder.

"Well, I'm going to buy Mr. Fargo a nice hot cup of coffee and then we can swap everything we've found out about the mysterious Mr. Brody."

"Halloway," Fargo said, turning to the sheriff.

"Where'd you get Halloway?"

"Steamboat office."

"He came in on the steamboat?"

"That's what they told me over there."

"Looks like you're one up on me, Fargo," the lawman said, not sounding happy.

"Well, you're one up on me here. I'm sure Bernard didn't tell me anything he didn't tell you."

"Didn't tell him half as much, Sheriff," Bernard said nervously. "Not a tenth as much, Sheriff."

Fargo laughed. "Not one twenty-eighth as much, Sheriff."

"Let's go get that coffee," the lawman said. Then to Bernard, "Next time, keep your mouth shut."

"Yes, sir."

"And I don't care if it's only one-fiftieth of what you told me."

"Yes, sir."

9

Twice a day, Amy walked around her bank and said hello to her employees.

Her father had taught her that a business that served the public was successful only if its employees were treated fairly. Amy had recently put a complaint box in the back room where the employees took their breaks.

The box had been there for two weeks now but there hadn't been any complaints. As much as Amy had assured them all that notes could be stuck in there with complete anonymity, the employees were still afraid they might get caught and be fired.

Amy made the late-morning sweep of the bank, personally greeting each employee and reminding them all that they should make use of the complaint box.

"You're really doing me and the bank a favor," she now explained to Glenda Rowlins. "That's the only way I can improve the bank and myself. I need people who can tell me what I'm doing wrong."

She knew the other tellers were listening so she glanced at them. "You don't have to make them real angry or anything. I'd like them to be polite, just the way I try to be polite to all of you. But say what's on your mind. I haven't even checked the box lately. I gave it up after the first eight days."

"Too bad Tom Minner retired," Glenda said. "That's about all he was good at—complaining."

Amy said, "I was thinking that myself." She grinned. "Old Tom would have kept that box stuffed every day." Then: "Well, don't forget what I said, everybody. Use that box."

She spent the next fifteen minutes talking to three different customers, good customers who helped form the backbone of the bank.

She was just headed back to her office when Mal Pickett came through the front door. He was an hour late, which irritated her. She didn't like tardiness unless there was a damned good excuse.

He wore a khaki shirt and trousers, and a snappy campaign hat rode his bald skull. He'd retired from the army a year ago and gone to work as her troubleshooter. But he still wanted to look like regular issue army. It was his identity.

"Ship was late, Amy. Sorry."

"You off-load the shipment yet?"

"I put four guards on it but the money's still aboard."

"Why didn't you off-load it?"

"I'm adding two men."

"Why?"

"We go to your office and talk?" He took off his hat and glanced around. "Private business."

They walked back to her office but she stopped at the room where people ate their lunches and took their breaks. She decided that after talking up the complaint box she should check to see if anybody'd actually dropped anything in it for her.

She was surprised to find a piece of regular writing paper that had been folded several times. She opened the shoebox and took out the paper, and carried it back to her office. The complaint was one she could easily fix. It read: *"Mrs. McGowan—our best customer—wants our coffee to be stronger."*

After the door was closed, when Mal was in his chair and she in hers, she said, "I hate mysteries, Mal. Tell me what's going on."

"I've got a feeling about this one."

"A feeling?"

"A bad one. There'll be more than sixty thousand dollars in those two stagecoaches we'll be drivin' up to the fort tomorrow."

She frowned. "You've got enough extra men to start a war."

"Not the kind of experienced men I need."

"Well, that's an odd thing to say, Mal. You're the one who hired them for my stage line."

"That's just it. The men we've got are fine for most stage runs. But they're not gunnies."

"Why would we need gunnies?"

"Because I talked to that colonel at the fort. He's convinced one of his men got his hands on the shipping orders. Time, place, route. He's sure that somebody snuck into his office at night and copied the orders."

"Why doesn't he send us some extra soldiers, then?"

Mal was rarely contemptuous but he snorted now. "Amy, think about it. If they have to supply their own security force, what are they hiring us for?"

"I guess you've got a good point."

Then she said, "Wait a minute. I've got a man for you. His name's Fargo."

"He tough?"

"He could whip two of you, Mal."

Mal was the kind of professional soldier who subjugated his pride to the job. He wanted to succeed and that meant using men who were tougher than him.

"Then he'd be just what I'm looking for. I need a man like that on the ship tonight. And then along on the trip tomorrow."

"One man could make that much difference?"

"If he's as tough as you say he is. That way I can run the coach up front and he can run the coach in back. And tonight he can sit on deck with a shotgun. He can trade shifts with two men so he gets some sleep and so do they. But he's on hand if they need him. Where can I find him?"

"Try the café. It's the middle of the day. If he isn't there, try his hotel." She named the hotel and room number. "Tell him you work for me, and tell him that we'll make this very much worth his while."

"We lose this one, we'll look pretty bad, Amy. And your friend Crowley would like nothing better."

Martin Crowley was the wealthiest man in this part of the Territory. His Sterling Stage line had pretty much sewn up its share of the Territory upriver. It had good coaches and experienced people and reasonable rates. But Crowley—for as much as Amy and Martin liked each other personally—had expansion plans. His boast was that they'd never lost a coach or a shipment. He was setting up a small office about thirty miles from here. He was cutting rates to attract some of Amy's customers. Losing a shipment of sixty thousand dollars sure wouldn't be good for Amy's reputation, especially with Martin already making his move for this part of the Territory.

"Find Fargo," she said. "And bring him back here."

Mal was glad that his boss finally shared his anxiety about this particular stage run. There was a hell of a lot at stake here.

10

Every once in a while they tried to pretend that they liked each other. But that never lasted for long.

Nick Crowley, who by virtue of size, good looks and pure meanness was the boss, said, "We'll leave here just after sundown."

"Why so early?" Hap Sievers said.

"I think even you could figure that out, Sievers, if you'd quit drinking that rotgut and think about it with that so-called brain of yours."

"Hey," Allie Blaine said. She was as small as she was pretty. Even in scruffy trail clothes, she was fetching. "I thought you were going to leave him alone."

A young woman and a drunk. A different kind of man would have been able to line up a much better pair of robbers. But Nick Crowley, son of the richest man in this part of the Territory, and the most abusive SOB west of the Mississippi, had to take what he could get. He had drunk, punched, stomped, shot, betrayed, humiliated and cheated away every friendship he'd made in his twenty-three years. He was left with the girl he was currently screwing and a pathetic would-be gambler as his cohorts. His old man had cut him off from any money three months ago, after the time he'd beaten up a respectable woman who wouldn't sleep with him because she was married. Nick had been drunk, of course, and couldn't remember much of it.

Now he was reduced to robbery and it was all the old man's fault. He thought bitterly of his pissant brother, Roger—so righteous, so hardworking, so honorable—and took satisfaction in remembering that the old man, drinking his bourbon one night, had said, "You're my favorite, Nick. I'm glad you didn't turn out like that brother of yours, even though he runs my businesses pretty damned well. Hell, the most exciting thing he's ever done was take those clarinet lessons his mother signed him up for. I don't want any son of mine to take clarinet lessons. I want him to be like you. Big and tough and a hellion with the ladies. But you've got to settle down some, son. I don't mind if you live it up. But there's limits to everything. I want you to go to work for me and really apply yourself. You pick the type of job you want and it's yours. And then I want you to mend some fences. You've made a lot of enemies in town. Wouldn't hurt at all that you deal out a few hands of apologies. You don't have to mean them but I think it's damned well time you say them. That's just how the game is played, son. Now I expect you to heed what I say."

But of the entire sermon, the only thing that Nick recalled with any passion was the old man making fun of Roger and his stupid clarinet lessons.

He sure hadn't changed his behavior any.

"The big thing is taking the guards out," Crowley said. "And that means distracting them with that little show you're gonna put on, Allie."

"I still think it'd be easier to just kill 'em," Sievers said.

They were camped outside town. None of them were what you'd call woodsmen, so the idea of shooting a rabbit and making it edible over a campfire was something they could only joke about. For this trip Allie had made some pretty darned good bread, which they ate in slices along with jerky. They'd agreed that they'd celebrate with a good meal after the robbery was over and that they were back home.

"You hear what he just said, Allie?" Crowley laughed.

"I heard." She shook her head. "Sievers, listen. There's gonna be a whole lot of people lookin' for us as it is. Just because we stole so much of their money. If we kill anybody while we're at it, that just means they'll put even more people on the job of findin' us. Is that so hard to figure out?"

"Maybe it'll come to that," Sievers said, unwilling to give up his argument. "Maybe we won't have no choice. Maybe we'll have to kill somebody."

"You kill anybody, Sievers, and I'll kill you," Crowley said, "and right on the spot. You hear me?"

"I hear you," Sievers said. "But if I have to kill somebody to save my own skin, that's just what I plan to do. And nothin' you say is gonna stop me."

And all Crowley could think of was how had he ever sunk so low that he was working with a trigger-happy moron like Sievers?

The meeting with Sheriff McLeod didn't amount to much.

Fact: Somebody had elected to shoot at Fargo last night.

Fact: Fargo had killed the man last night.

Fact: The man signed on the steamboat manifest as Earl Halloway, and at the hotel as Earl Brody.

Fact: They didn't know a damned thing about him, otherwise.

"Why would he want to kill you?" Sheriff McLeod asked, blowing on his steaming cup of coffee.

"No idea."

"Could he have gotten you confused with somebody else?"

"He knew who I was. He followed me out to Amy's place and then waited for me in the woods, knowing I'd probably take the same road back to town."

"He couldn't be anybody from your past? I reckon you've made a lot of enemies with that gun of yours."

"I'm pretty sure I've never seen him before."

"So we don't know his name for sure. We don't know why he came here. We don't know if he's a hired gun or he just had it in for you. And if he's a hired gun, then who hired him to come here?"

"I'll add one more to your list, McLeod."

"Good. That's just what we need. One more thing we can't figure out."

"He got here a day before I did. Nobody had any idea

I was stopping here. I didn't have any idea. I just stopped because I thought sleeping on a mattress sounded good."

"So he didn't come here to kill you?"

"He didn't even know I existed when he came here."

"But there was a change of plans. If somebody hired him to come here, then they wanted him to kill somebody else. But then, for some reason, this Brody or whatever the hell his real name is was told to kill you first."

The day was rolling toward noon. The café was starting to fill up. The clamor and clatter of people being served, along with the unceasing drone of voices, made it difficult to talk without half shouting. And neither man wanted to shout. The man who'd brought Brody here might be sitting nearby.

"We've got a mystery on our hands, Sheriff."

McLeod reached for his hat. "Two years from now I'll be retired and none of this will make any difference at all. Anybody else shoots at you, Fargo, you let me know."

"You'll be the first, Sheriff"—Fargo put on his own hat—"unless he kills me, of course."

11

Nick Crowley rode downriver with his binoculars to take a look at the small, almost tuglike craft that had brought the money, dry goods and medicines to the dock on the edge of town.

Allie and Sievers stayed behind.

Allie contented herself with walking through the nearby

woods. In an informal way, she studied nature, identifying birds, trees, flowers, bushes. She'd asked Sievers if he wanted to go along. He'd just scoffed at her.

When she got back to the campsite, she saw that Sievers had managed to find another pint of rye somewhere. Nick had taken his other one so Sievers couldn't drink any more. The robbery was less than five hours away.

"Nick isn't going to be happy."

"Nick won't know unless you tell him, Allie."

"I hate to tell you this but it's pretty easy to tell when you're drunk."

"I'm just steadyin' my nerves is all. I won't get drunk. I got more self-control than that."

She didn't want to hurt his feelings by saying anything. He spent most of his pay on gambling. Everybody in town knew that his wife threatened to leave six, seven times a year, and take the kids with her. She took in wash and did sewing for rich people and scrubbed floors when she had to. If it was up to him, the family would starve.

He had a lot of self-control, all right.

She followed the flight of a hawk riding a wind. In a couple of days she'd be just as free as that hawk was. She'd have enough for her train ticket to Chicago and she'd go there and get herself lost and nobody in these parts would ever hear from her again. She was young, smart, pretty. She felt sure that all sorts of adventures awaited her. She wasn't naive enough to think that she was going to meet some foreign prince or anything like that. But she did feel sure that she would marry well and have a nice big house and a few nice big children.

"You trust him?"

His words knocked her from her perch of daydreams. "What?"

"Crowley. You trust him?"

"About the same as I trust you."

"I think he's gonna kill us and take off with the money."

She couldn't help it. She giggled. She sounded eight years old when she did it—a pure, little, sweet, girly sound.

"What's so damn funny?"

"That's what he told me about you."

"Bullshit."

"Bullshit yourself. That's exactly what he said."

"He just wants you to throw in with him so he'll have you on his side when he cuts me out of my share."

She lay back, hands behind her head.

He looked at her appreciatively. Long time since he'd had sex with his old woman. She wasn't much more than bone and sinew now, anyway. And anyway, she wanted nothing to do with him. Only stayed with him because she wouldn't be able to support the kids unless she had the few dollars she managed to get from him after he'd blown most of his pay on poker.

But Allie here, those proper little breasts of hers and that rich shapely ass of hers—Lord, he could imagine himself inside her and grinding away as he gripped her buttocks, her bucking and bucking and bucking as they both drove blind and hollering and half-crazed to their finish.

And he'd keep going. He knew he would. He wouldn't rest more than a few minutes and she'd be startled by how hard he was when he slipped into her juices and the softest little spot ever known to mankind. Maybe they'd take it a little easier this time, him bringing her nipples erect so he could chew them gently, driving her right back into her own need for another go at it. And then he'd turn her over so that she was riding him, fulfilling herself on the sheath of his manhood, once again his big hands on that royal ass of hers, driving her harder and harder so he went as deep as you could go, her thrusting up and down, up and down, up and down the whole time. Until she finally fell forward, spent, her face tucked into his neck, and the luxurious after-feeling of still being inside her soft, sweet, moist treasure.

"How the heck did we ever get together?" she said, staring up at the sky. "I don't trust you or him, you don't trust him or me, and neither me nor Nick trusts you. I don't think that's how something like this is supposed to work."

"It is pretty damn strange when you think about it."

"We all need money. That's the only thing we have in common."

"Money. And a lot of it . . . You know, Allie, me'n you could throw in together and kill him and take his cut."

She hooted at that one. "Of course you and Nick could throw in together and kill me and take my cut."

"You know I wouldn't do nothing like that to you, Allie."

"Oh, sure," she said. "An honorable man like you wouldn't ever do anything like that, now, would you? Just shut up for a while. I want to take a nap."

But he was already back to coveting her with the very essence of his being, his manhood pulsing with such force that he thought he'd have a heart attack if he couldn't plunge it into her right here and right now.

12

Mal Pickett said, "I'll be glad to pay you half down now if you'd like, Fargo."

"Let's wait and make sure everything goes all right."

Pickett and Fargo had checked the boat out. It was a small cargo craft with a storage area in its center where several hundred pounds of merchandise were stacked under tightly cinched tarpaulins. It was easy to defend in that you could see anybody approaching. Of course, with only three men—two soldiers had brought the craft here—a gang could make guarding the money difficult. The plan was to load the stagecoaches just before dawn and strike out then. Taking the money to the bank for the night and then taking it out again would give any would-be robbers two opportunities to strike at a vulnerable time. The stagecoaches would be surrounded by men. It would have to be a formidable gang to steal the money. The loss of life on both sides would be heavy.

"Well, if you're comfortable here, Fargo, I guess I might as well head back to town." Pickett put his hand out and the men shook.

After Pickett left, Fargo walked over to where the two blue-uniformed soldiers sat playing cards.

Fargo said, "I get a couple hours' sleep, I'll be fine. And I don't care when it is. You boys decide what'll be best for you."

The one named Fisher, a towheaded kid with a fierce scar down his left cheek, said, "I guess we were kind of figuring that we'd take the early shifts sleeping and then spell you about one a.m. or so."

"Fine by me."

"You really expecting trouble?" Ransom, the hick-sounding one, said.

"Hard to tell. This'd be the most logical place for them to attack, if they're going to."

Ransom said, "We're always totin' money—sometimes a lot more than this—on the river. Robbers don't expect the army to use little boats like this with so many greenbacks. We ain't been robbed yet and it's been three years."

"Almost four," Fisher said.

"It's the big ships they hit," Ransom said.

"Well, then, I guess I can look forward to a nice, long, boring night, which would be right nice by me."

Fargo gave them a nod and went forward. He jumped onto the dock. He'd covered the nearby area with Mal Pickett, who was a solid professional. The men had located the trouble spots where robbers might hide. A ragged stand of hardwoods was where they'd likely come from.

Only now did Fargo realize he was hungry. His last food had been at the café with the sheriff. A long time ago. Well, he had some jerky in his saddlebags and that would hold him over. Jerky and water had seen him through some mighty long spells on the lonely and sometimes dangerous trails where the myth of the Trailsman played out.

Convinced that he'd now memorized the hiding places any robbers were likely to use, Fargo turned and looked at the violet twilight and the stars burning in the endless sky. Nights on water were usually good ones for Fargo. The water relaxed him, nourished him in a way that land rarely did.

He was actually going to enjoy his spell riding shotgun on this boat tonight.

That was because he didn't know what lay ahead.

13

When Nick Crowley returned to camp, he found Allie and Sievers sitting far apart. Obviously the two hadn't worked up any great friendship during his absence.

Or was that what they wanted him to think by looking so standoffish? Were they plotting to help him steal the money and then turn against him? He didn't trust Sievers at all. And Allie was young and vulnerable; she might be led by Sievers to betray Nick.

Crowley had a moment when he wondered if he shouldn't forget this and ride on. But ride on to where? He had no money, he had no skills. At twenty-three he was as helpless as a ten-year-old. He'd lived off his father all his life.

He could see an early silvering of frost on the darkening ground. He'd told them not to build a fire. But now he wished he could sit Indian-legged next to a small blaze and warm his hands and smell coffee heating up.

Sievers was sleeping, or doing a good imitation of it. In the early, fragile moonlight, Crowley saw the glint of the pint bottle. The bastard had held out on him. Needless to say, the bottle was empty.

He stalked over to Allie.

"Hi, Nick."

"Why'd you let him get drunk?"

"You may not have noticed but he's got seventy pounds on me and he can be a very mean man when he wants to be." Allie stood up. She'd been resting against a tree, and now she wiped chunks of autumn leaves from her very sweet bottom. "We'll have to sober him up."

Nick had slept with her several times in recent months. She wasn't new anymore—not new to him, anyway; new to somebody else, yes, but that wasn't his concern—and he had no interest in her now except as somebody who'd help him get his hands on that money. "And just how do you propose to do that, little girl?"

"Don't call me that!" she snapped. "You know how much I hate that."

"Well, then, just how are you going to do that?"

She raised a delicate hand and pointed south. "Did you happen to notice that small lake over there? We throw him in there naked. That water must be damned near freezing."

"And what if that doesn't work?"

"It will work, Nick. Damn. You've gotta calm down. Won't do any good to have you all crazy like this."

"Yeah, well I've got good reason to be crazy. We're supposed to swing out of here in a few minutes."

"He'll be ready. If you help me carry him to the lake."

A few minutes later, next to the small circle of lake that the moonlight had hammered into a silver coin, they stripped him buck naked and then lifted him and threw him into the water.

Near as Allie could figure, the water was nearly waist deep. But deep enough to do what it needed to.

Not even a minute later, the cursing, spluttering, hairy figure of Sievers reappeared.

The cursing must have gone on a full minute during which Sievers accused the two of them of every crime known to man, except maybe having sex with a mule.

They stood back and let him make his way out.

He was shivering so badly that they couldn't understand

any of his swear words. All they heard from him was the very real sound of his teeth clattering.

"I'd say he was ready," she said.

"I'd have to agree."

"Where're my clothes, you skunks?"

"To your left, Sievers," Nick said.

"I'll get pneumonia and die, like my mother did that spring."

He quit bitching long enough to go get his clothes. He stood bare assed so, in case she was interested, Allie couldn't get a peek at his privates. He wasn't all that well endowed and that really wasn't her business. She'd just spread lies about him. And it. Everybody spread lies about him.

When Sievers was dressed again, Nick Crowley said, "We're late now. Let's ride out of here."

But now, under Crowley's angry stare, Sievers spoke up nervously.

"It wasn't my fault, Nick. I swear. She shoulda stopped me, Nick. She shoulda taken the bottle from me. It was her responsibility. It really was."

Now Allie was glaring at him, too. "You're pathetic, sometimes," she said. "You know that, Sievers? Just downright pathetic."

14

She came to him from the deep dusk, an apparition. And the closer she got, the wider his smile became. Even though he wasn't the settling-down kind, he had come to like Amy in a way he'd liked few women. The marrying kind.

He stood up from the chair he'd planted so he could see the entire sweep of the dock. The river was churning tonight, so he had to stiffen his legs. Been awhile since he'd felt the pitch of a boat beneath him.

She was dressed in a white blouse and butternuts. She carried, both hands beneath it, a large plate that was covered with a length of cloth. The way she bore it seemed almost reverent, like a sacrifice or offering.

They both started grinning at the same time. She was obviously as happy to see him as he was to see her.

"Have you eaten supper yet?"

"I had some mighty tasty jerky."

"How about some mighty tasty slices of turkey with a boiled potato and green beans, and a nice slice of apple pie?"

"You think I'd eat something like that when I've got jerky?"

"You're quite the comedian, Fargo."

"Not in bed, I hope."

"You're just fishing for compliments."

"Well, I'm on a boat, aren't I? Might as well fish for something."

And then he met her on the dock and they both managed to find each other's lips even though she still held the plate. He felt a lot happier to see her than he wanted to. If a fella wasn't careful, a fella could start feelin' a whole lot of things he didn't want to. Not if he wanted to keep his freedom, anyway.

And then dock became boat and she sat watching him hungrily destroy every molecule of food on that poor, defenseless plate.

"You're the kind of man a woman likes to cook for."

"How come?" he said between gulps.

"The way you appreciate food. You keep yourself on the slim side. You work hard and save yourself for a small amount of food. Gluttons just eat to fill the void. You have a real appreciation for food."

"I have a real appreciation for this food, anyway. Thanks again for the grub. You're sure a good cook."

She smiled. "Well, I have to be honest. My maid cooked it for you."

"Yeah, but it wouldn't taste half as good if you hadn't delivered it."

This time the smile became a gentle laugh. "Flatterer."

"Damned right. I want some more of her cookin' and your deliverin' sometime."

That was when the screams came.

15

Make it sound good. Make it sound real.

Those were the thoughts in Allie's head as she waited for Sievers to fire two shots in the air.

Then she was to scream. As planned.

But what if she didn't scream loud enough? Or what if it sounded fake?

She could barely see Sievers behind her.

But then she saw the barrel of his rifle gleam in the moonlight and she let go with the scream.

And then she began running through the shallow stand of trees to the clearing in front of the dock.

Her next move was to stumble and fall down as if she was wounded, or already dead.

The falling down proved easier than the screaming.

Fargo was one with his Colt. He wasn't aware of snapping it from his holster, or even filling his hand with it.

"She looks like she's dead," Amy said. She didn't sound like Amy. All that cool self-control was gone, at least for now. Panic and terror. Crazy time.

Fargo knew this could be a setup. He turned and shouted to the soldiers on the other side of the stacked cargo, "One of you get up here and cover Amy!"

Then he jumped from the boat to the dock and started moving fast toward the girl, his eyes scanning the trees for any sign that this was some kind of ruse to distract him away from the boat.

The girl wasn't moving.

He got down on one knee when he reached her. His left hand worked her neck for a sign of a pulse. His eyes stayed on the woods she had fled from.

Her pulse was so strong he knew instantly that he had been pulled away from the boat by a very effective ruse.

He had time for this thought and no more before the girl jumped up from the ground and hurled herself at him, catching him in an awkward position where he couldn't keep his balance.

She rode him down to the ground, struggling with him to take his Colt from his hand. She was slight but amazingly quick and strong. She also was a master with her fingernails and right knee. She got him twice in the groin with expert dispatch.

"Skye!" Amy shouted from the boat. "He's coming toward you!"

Then there came the crack of a rifle. Then two, three cracks.

In the darkness, in the sweaty bone-pain of wrestling with this girl, in the confusion over the shots—where were they coming from and whose rifle was at work?—he heard Amy scream again. Only this time it was the quality of the scream that shocked him. The scream of the mortally wounded. He'd seen plenty of death in his days. He'd also heard plenty of death. It had an unmistakable shocked sound to it. Body telling brain that they were both dying. The shock coming from the brain first trying to deny this terrible knowledge; and then from the horror of accepting it—the entire process taking no more than a second or two.

A few more shots. These—from what he could imagine rather than see—from behind the cargo.

But he didn't give a damn about that now. All he was concerned with was Amy.

He brought an uppercut to the girl's chin with such force

48

that he could hear her teeth shatter, and then he flung her aside.

Amy. Had to get to Amy.

He had been so busy struggling to his feet that he hadn't seen the silhouetted figure standing a yard away with the rifle.

Amy. Had to get to Amy.

"You take one more step, mister, and I'll kill you."

Somewhere to Fargo's side, the girl spoke through her bloody mouth. "No killin'. That was what we agreed to, Sievers. No killin'."

But Fargo couldn't stand there any longer.

Get to Amy. Get to Amy.

It was an irrational thought given that Fargo had lost his Colt somewhere in the struggle. No way of defending himself. And even more irrational considering that a man was holding a rifle on him.

But he wasn't rational right now. Too much rage, too much fear. Thinking clearly didn't matter anymore. There was just this deep animal need to save Amy, to protect Amy—feelings so unknown to Fargo that they overwhelmed him and he had no choice but to obey their call.

Fargo stumbled on. And if he hadn't stumbled, the first bullet from Sievers's rifle would have cleaved his head in half. But Sievers wasn't done. He'd show the bastard that he couldn't get away. Not from a man as tough as Sievers. No, sir.

So the next bullet did what no other bullet had ever done to Skye Fargo. It took a sizable chunk out of the right side of his head. Tore it out as if a big serrated knife had ripped into Fargo's skull.

He had almost reached the boat and was able to see, in the last few moments of consciousness, the body of Amy slung across the bow of the boat, frozen in the exact spot where she'd fallen after the bullets had taken her life. Nearby, one of the soldiers lay dead.

Did he say, "Amy!" or did he only think it?

He would never be sure, of course.

Never.

16

"Your name is Fargo."

"Fargo?"

"Yes. Skye Fargo."

"Skye Fargo? That doesn't sound right."

"You nearly died. You've been in this bed right here for two weeks."

"Two weeks? That's a long time."

"That's an even longer time when you're a doctor and waiting to see if your patient is ever going to recover."

"My head—it hurts a lot."

"You should be dead. I think the Lord Almighty saved you for a reason. I know docs don't like to mix religion much with medicine but if you want my opinion, that's my feeling."

"My arms and legs work all right."

"Yes. But you've lost ten pounds or better, and you're going to be weak as hell until you get back to eating regular. And even then you're going to be wobbly for a while."

Fargo glanced around the room. About as big as a cell. Except it had a window. A branch full of red-and-gold autumn leaves scraped the glass. And because the window was open a few inches, a smoky fall breeze that soothed his pounding head slipped elegantly into the room. There was a crucifix on one wall and a framed photograph of the president on the other.

"You remember anything about that night?" the doc

said. He was young, maybe midtwenties, with a pock-marked face and long, graceful hands that didn't show much hard physical labor.

"Which night would that be?"

"The night you got shot."

Fargo laid his head back on the pillow plumped up at the head of the single bed.

"Guess I don't."

"You remember a woman named Amy?"

Amy. Faintly, as if calling from another universe, the name filled his seething mind. But—no. No real recollection of any Amy. "Guess I don't remember that, either."

"Well, she was killed and the money was taken."

"I knew this Amy?"

"That's the way the people at the bank tell it. She owned the bank. You were working for her. But a couple of the people who worked there thought you were maybe friends, if you know what I mean by that. Good friends. She was a beautiful woman."

"And she's dead."

"Yes. Dead and buried. So were the two soldiers who were helping you guard the money on the boat."

Fargo heard this story with great interest but no particular feelings. A beautiful woman. Money. Dead soldiers. A boat. His name was Fargo—or so this young doc said.

"What happens now?"

"Well, tomorrow I'm going to let the sheriff come and visit you. He's been hounding me. But you didn't come out of your coma until today. And now you have amnesia, though I don't expect it'll last too long. A head wound like you have, amnesia isn't exactly unheard of. But I want you to get some strength back before the law starts working on you with questions. And I'd better give you some warning."

"What kind of warning?"

"People probably won't believe you when you tell them you can't remember anything."

"Why not?"

The doc shrugged. "It's just the way people are. Since they've never experienced it, they just don't see how it's possible to forget your name and what happened to you."

"I remember some things when I was a little boy. I can

see a farm and I can see people. I think that's me and my boyhood anyway. But I don't know their names or anything."

"Not uncommon. A lot of amnesia is just forgetting things that happened in a specific period of time."

"But mine seems—"

The doc nodded. "Yours is a lot more severe. If it follows true to form, you'll be remembering little things as you go along and then one day everything'll fall in place."

"Like getting hit on the head. I remember reading about that."

The doc grinned. "That makes for a good story. And it happens, but maybe you'll see something or somebody that reminds you of an incident you can't quite place, and then it'll be there—everything."

"It sounds like nobody knows much about it."

"You're right about that, Mr. Fargo. We just go along with it more than anything. Maybe someday there'll be a patent medicine bottle that works on it. But for right now—"

Fargo yawned. "I guess you're right. I sure don't seem to have much strength."

"That's why I'm keeping the law off you for another day. You get some rest now. And when you get up my wife'll be here to feed you a real good meal. Including pumpkin pie."

Fargo grinned with lips so dry they looked like ancient parchment. "Now that'll be worth waking up for." Then he added, "Have I been dreaming, or do you actually have a beautiful nurse called Rhonda?"

The young doc grinned. "She's as curious about you as you are about her. She gave you a good washing yesterday and said she can't wait till you can stand up." The grin got wider. "Seems you're a mighty big man in a couple different ways."

Fargo let the compliment cheer him up for a moment. But as his eyes closed and he felt himself edging up to the abyss of sleep, the cheer died quickly.

He hoped that when he fell asleep he would have a dream that would bring everything back to him. The beautiful woman. The boat. The money.

And the bastard who'd taken half of Fargo's head off.

17

The sheriff introduced himself as McLeod. He had a badge that had to be a burden to carry around. It was not only big, it looked solid. It covered most of the upper lapel of his dark suit.

"Doc tells me you don't remember anything."

"Not anything that would help you or me, anyway."

"You coulda been a part of it."

"Coulda. But I woulda had a hell of a time shootin' myself in the head that way."

"Maybe."

"Maybe?" Fargo snorted. "Maybe? I damned near died. You don't fake a wound like that. You shoot yourself in the arm or leg."

"You seem to know a lot about fake wounds."

Fargo tried to shake his head. The lance of pain severing his skull reminded him to keep his head as still as possible. "I'm kinda disappointed in you, Sheriff."

"Yeah? And why would that be?"

"You're not as smart as you look."

"Very funny." He rocked back on his heels and said, "One thing you didn't forget."

"How to piss off lawmen?"

McLeod had to laugh at that one. "Exactly. Doc tells me you have a headache something fierce." He leaned in and rapped his knuckles hard against Fargo's skull. "Hope it gives ya a lot more pain before it gets better."

"I saw what he did to you," the nurse named Rhonda said, appearing seconds after the lawman left. She came over to him, adjusted his covers and leaned in to place her right hand on his forehead to test his temperature.

As she drew closer, her breasts pressed against his arm and, even in his poor condition, he felt life come to his crotch.

She must have felt his whole body stir because she winked at him and said, "Much pain as you're in, Mr. Fargo, I'd think you'd want to rest."

"Maybe I could just lie here and you could attack me."

"You're probably a virgin."

"That's right." He smiled. "That's why you have to be gentle with me."

"I could probably ease myself up on top of you."

"What about the doc?"

"He has to go to a meeting. Fact is, I think he already left." She then proceeded to perform a miracle. In seconds, she was naked.

"I didn't think anybody could undress that fast," Fargo said.

"I can when I want to."

"And you want to?"

"Very much."

She eased his blanket off him, eased up the nightshirt he wore and said, "A nice big one. Yummy."

She gently pushed him back on the bed, stroking his lust spear while kissing his now-naked chest and nipples. She worked her way down until she was right up against the swollen head of his desire, and then she began to run her tongue up and down its length, fondling his testicles at the same time.

He was in such ecstasy that he was barely aware of her easing herself upward and then mounting him, her own juices already plentiful and hot. She did two things at once—began riding him and leaned forward so that he could ravish the huge brown nipples of her breasts.

He was surprised at his own strength, his hands iron on her buttocks as he drove her harder and harder against him. They started kissing with such insane fury that they almost pushed each other off the narrow bed.

And then in a conjoining of genitals and needs, they became as one, welded together long enough to share the explosion that each felt simultaneously.

She collapsed on him and he didn't mind at all.

"I'm not sure that's part of the recovery process," she giggled breathlessly.

"Well, if it isn't," Fargo said, sliding his hand up and down her sweat-slick back, "it should be."

18

The town of Lattimore in Dakota Territory was located forty miles due south of where that vast volcanic prehistoric rock pile known as the Badlands began. Given its location, it had quickly become the commercial hub for the area, especially for farmers. Sometimes it got a little too proud of the fact that it had two two-story buildings and a link to a railroad, but in fact it was just the sort of place that surprised Easterners who thought all Western towns were basically large outhouses.

Fargo reached there wearing new duds, riding an Ovaro stallion that displayed a loyalty to the big man that was downright touching and carrying in his back pocket a letter written on the letterhead of the doc who'd treated him, testifying to the fact that Fargo suffered from amnesia. Fargo was to present this to a doc in Lattimore.

His Colt and his Henry were with him because the lawman back downtrail had gone to Fargo's hotel room and given the Trailsman everything that belonged to him. In addition to the firearms, that included clothes, money and a yellow telegraph wire about an old friend of Fargo's who was dying.

Fargo had come to Lattimore for a simple reason. The liveryman who handled Amy's stagecoach horses had been asked by Sheriff McLeod to look at some of the hoofprints the killers had left behind. The liveryman noted that one of the horses had shoes bearing nails with an octagonal head on them. These were used in this part of the Territory only by a liveryman in Lattimore, the next town over. Most blacksmiths felt that this new type of nail didn't go in as clean as the older kind. They had a tendency to bend.

With no further memories of the night of the robbery, and no other lead than the hoofprints, Fargo had decided to ride to Lattimore to investigate on his own. The town would also lead him to where his old friend was lying gravely ill.

Fargo found a hotel, checked in and slept. He was still weak.

When he woke up, he went for a walk around town. The crisp autumn wind revived him. He felt better, stronger, more purposeful than he had since waking up from the coma.

If he could just remember things that pertained to the robbery and the killings. All sorts of other memories popped up. He could see them clearly. The trouble was he couldn't remember who the people were. Or how he knew them. Or, of course, who he was and how he fit into these tableaus.

He almost tried to find a doc and give him the letter he carried from the other doc. Maybe this new doc knew something about amnesia that the other one hadn't.

But for the time being anything remotely connected to medicine was to be avoided. He liked just walking around the town, enjoying the sight of pretty ladies, peering into store windows, and looking at all the fancy new vehicles that joined the rumbling old wagons in keeping the main street jammed with traffic.

He enjoyed being a part of the human flow—even if he didn't have any idea of who the hell he was.

He was just crossing the main street to check in with the

sheriff, when he felt somebody staring at him intently. When he looked around at the faces to his right, he saw one whose eyes seemed fixed on him—the eyes of a wispy but pretty young woman in a blue winter sweater and denims. He sensed she recognized him. He had no idea who she was.

He had gotten no farther than the middle of the street before the young woman had taken off, moving in a trot down the board sidewalk.

Nick Crowley said, "Another whiskey, Merle."

The saloon was empty except for a pair of drunks sleeping it off at different tables. They were snoring so loudly, it was as if they were in a contest.

"That's number three, Nick."

"I know that's number three," Nick said. "And I don't give a shit if it's number three. Now I asked for a whiskey and by God I'd better get it."

"You know what your old man told me. You get drunk and get into trouble, he's gonna hold me personally responsible."

"To hell with my old man. I want a drink and I want it now."

"Can't do it, Nick. You were half drunk when you came in here. I sure don't want to go up against your old man." Then he said, "Hey, what the hell? You can't come in here."

Allie frowned, standing just inside the batwings. "I need to talk to Nick."

"Then, Nick, I'd suggest you go outside."

"Not till I have that drink."

The bartender sighed. The owner had a strict "No Female" policy. The other saloons all had dance-hall girls working in them, but the owner here thought it was unseemly to have women in saloons—they should be home cooking up delights for their families, taking care of their kids and eagerly awaiting the opportunity to pop out a few more babies. They sure as hell shouldn't be in saloons.

"This is important, Nick."

Nick winked at the bartender. "Everything with her is important."

Allie's temper lashed out at him. "Listen, you souse. If I say it's important, it's important. Now you haul your ass outside so we can talk."

"You watch your language," the bartender said. He didn't cotton to women who used bad language. His momma had never used bad language.

Nick's reputation was that of a man who always had at least one woman throwing herself at him. But this wasn't one of them. This was a woman who was sick of his self-indulgence and special treatment, just because he was the son of the Territory's richest man.

The bartender said, "Maybe you should go outside with her, Nick."

"Not without that drink."

"Give him his drink, mister. And give it to him now. And, Nick, meet me in the town square."

The bartender sneered at her. "You gonna beat me up if I don't give him that drink?"

"You'd be surprised, you ugly old fart," she said. "Now give him his drink."

"Bitch," the man muttered to himself.

But he gave Nick Crowley his drink.

19

"Guess you should read this, too, Sheriff," Doc Grimes said. His red suspenders were almost as red as his whiskey nose. He wore spectacles that magnified his hangover blue eyes.

As Sheriff Cordell read the letter through, Grimes said, "Never personally ran into this before."

"Neither have I," Fargo said.

"Bet it's scary."

"Bet it's bullshit, is what I bet it is," Sheriff Cordell said. He looked New England with the long, gaunt face and the long, gaunt body and the celluloid collar inside his suit jacket. His badge was modest, as was the six-shooter strapped around his narrow waist. His hair was supposed to be white but it was streaked with yellow.

"No call to say that," Grimes said. "This here is an actual medical problem."

"That doesn't mean he's got it, though. He could be faking."

"I could be," Fargo said, reasonably enough, "but what would I get out of faking it?"

"You'd know more about that than I would," the lawman said, still irritable. To Grimes, he said, "We don't even know he wrote this letter."

"Looks real enough to me."

"I'll be happy to send this doc a telegram," Fargo said.

"Now that sounds pretty good," Grimes said. "Unless you think he can find a way to send a telegram to himself."

"How do we know who is on the other end?"

Grimes smiled at Fargo. "You see the shit I have to put up with? I'd kick his ass out of here if he wasn't ten years younger and a lot stronger than I am."

"Maybe if you drank less than a quart of rotgut every day, you'd get some of your strength back."

"Least I didn't get the clap three times in one year."

Fargo laughed. "You two boys should be on the stage."

Grimes nodded, then got serious. He sat up straight in the chair in front of his rolltop desk. Through an open interior door his examination room could be seen. Everything but the examination table was white. The table was brown leather with a lot of padding for the patient's comfort. Fargo suspected that despite the man's love of alcohol, he was probably a pretty good doc and kept up with modern equipment. "So you were there when these three people got killed."

"That's what they tell me."

"And you took a bullet to the head that should've killed you."

"Sure did."

"But when you came out of the coma, you didn't remember that night."

"Nope. Didn't remember much except stray memories from different points in my life."

"So if you don't remember anything, Fargo, why'd you come here?" Grimes said.

Fargo shrugged. "The horse tracks. The kind of nails holding the shoes."

"Those octagonal ones Conrad uses over at the livery," Grimes said.

"A lot of blacksmiths use 'em," the sheriff said.

"Not in this part of the Territory," Fargo said. "At least, that's what I was told."

The lawman looked him over, then looked at the medical man. "So you think he really can't remember."

"I'm pretty sure he can't. This kind of thing isn't common, but it isn't uncommon, either. The letter says that Fargo here was very close to this Amy who was killed. One of the things in the medical books says that this kind of memory loss can be brought on by the patient not being able to face something terrible—so his mind forces him to forget. The other thing that can bring it on is an injury or wound to the head. Fargo here has had both of those things happen to him. He cared about the woman and somebody shot him in the right side of the head. That sure could bring it on." He paused. "By the way, Mr. Fargo, there's a gal doctor on the other side of the street about two blocks up. I'm leavin' on a train tomorrow and she'll be seein' my patients. We got a real nice relationship." He smiled. "Beautiful little Jewish gal. You'll like her just fine, believe me."

The sheriff pushed off the wall he'd been leaning against. He surprised Fargo by offering his hand. They shook. "I'll take the doc's word for things—temporarily. But you get into any trouble in this town, Fargo, and you're gonna have yourself one hell of an enemy, I can tell you that."

The lawman walked to the door. "And speaking of memory, yours is getting bad too, Grimes. I didn't have the clap three times in one year. I had it four times in one year."

Grimes laughed. "Yeah, I can see where you'd sure be proud of settin' a record like that."

In the dying day, the bandstand in the town square was a melancholy sight, especially to Allie, who loved music so much. Now the only sounds were Halloween leaves scraping across the empty stage where, under a summer moon, trumpets and violins and bright, smart pianos could be heard, the songs ranging from merry toe-tappers to sad romantic refrains. And to see half the town spread out around the front of the bandstand was almost as thrilling as the music itself.

Not the violet streaks of coming dusk, nor even the oddly sweet hooting of a nearby owl, not even the tender cries of mothers calling their little ones in for supper—the mothers always sounding just a bit nervous in the failing light, knowing that terrible things could happen to little ones—none of these could make Allie feel any better about the simple fact that almost never left her waking mind.

She had signed on to the robbery as a way of raising enough money to run off to Chicago and take on life as a city girl. She had a head full of magazine dreams, of true loves, of nights at the theater, of fancy carriages pulled by horses as sleek and black as midnight itself. Little-girl dreams.

She signed on knowing that they could be caught and that she'd be forced to serve time in prison, her little-girl dreams at least delayed, and possibly dashed forever.

But she had signed on with a firm understanding that there would be no violence. She realized now that Nick and Sievers were not men who could guarantee such a promise. They had terrible tempers. And so no guarantee could possibly hold.

She sat on the top step of the bandstand, Sievers on the bottom step.

"C'mon, Allie. Tell me. He's late. Hell, he might not even show up."

"You sound like a little kid, Sievers. Now just be quiet and let me listen to the birds."

They'd be headed south soon, the warm-weather birds, and Lord, didn't she envy them. Her mother had died when she was four and her father raised her until she was eleven, when he developed a variety of sicknesses that she had to tend to. It took him six long years to die and by that time she resented him for taking away her freedom. She'd had to quit school, work four hours a day washing dishes in the café, with no friends, no dances, not even sleighing in the winter when moonlight turned snow to blue diamonds—no life at all. Till now. Till the robbery money that would take her far away. But she should have known better. Three dead bodies. She'd been terrified enough these past days.

But now this new development . . .

Nick Crowley came striding across the town square with the swagger that never left him. He had looks for the ladies and a mean streak for the men. He was lusted after by women and feared by men. The only thing he didn't have was his old man's respect. Too much of a hellion. The old man had cut him off from money and shelter months ago. And so the boy who'd grown up so rich, so arrogant, so hated, was now just as flat busted as everybody else in this pitiless old world. The robbery had been his idea.

He stood in front of them now, hip cocked, one hand on the handle of his six-shooter, black pants, gray shirt, black vest, low-brimmed black hat. A dime-novel guy.

"What the hell do you think you're doing, coming into the saloon like that?" he snapped at Allie. "You sounded like the world's coming to an end or something."

"She won't tell me what's goin' on," Sievers said.

"I'll tell you now," she said, savoring the words she was about to speak, knowing that they would be shaken by them—scared, even if they wouldn't admit it. "He's in town."

"Who's in town?" Crowley said.

"The one Sievers here wounded in the head." A newspaper account had brought them up-to-date. Names of the dead and wounded.

"How the hell you know that?" Sievers said.

"Because I saw him."

"Bullshit," Crowley said. "You been so scared about it all, you just imagined you saw him."

"I got a good clear look at him, Nick," Allie said, half enjoying the smugness that was even now leaving him. "A good clear look. And there's only one reason he's here. To find us and turn us over to the law."

There was a silence—just her beloved birds—and then Crowley spoke. "You really got a good, clear look at him, Allie?"

"Yeah, Nick," she said. "He's really here."

20

"You're gonna be surprised who wants to see you, Mr. Fargo."

Fargo had just entered his hotel when the desk clerk, a plump and nervous man who gladly accepted the pity people gave him after a glance or two, said, "Mr. Crowley himself. Old Man Crowley."

"Old Man who?" Fargo asked, stopping at the front desk.

The clerk's pink right hand twitched. Some kind of spastic condition, Fargo thought. Poor bastard.

The clerk, sweaty and reeking of some kind of fancy barbershop skin juice, leaned forward and whispered, "The most important man in this part of the Territory."

"And he wants to see me?"

The clerk nodded. "He's waitin' in the hotel bar right over there. You can't miss him. He looks like an Old Testament prophet. And he's six and a half feet tall. People are terrified of him."

Crowley sounded hard to miss all right.

Then the clerk said, "Oh, the boy over to the telegraph shop brought this."

Even before he read the message, Fargo knew what it would say. And he was right:

SKYE—DAD DIED EARLY THIS MORNING. HE DIDN'T WANT FUNERAL. NO REASON TO COME HERE NOW.

—KAREN

Fargo thanked the desk clerk and headed for the bar.

One could find a better class of drunks in a saloon like this. The upper class of locals, of drummers, of con artists. Cons of every kind were tried here nightly because these customers had money or access to it. Fargo had learned long ago that, with his size and his scowl, he had no trouble keeping charlatans at bay.

Fargo and Crowley identified each other instantly, power of one kind recognizing power of another.

He was a striking old white-haired man of sixtysomething, Fargo guessed. Even sitting, there was about him an aura of competence, purpose and arrogance. When he waved for Fargo to come to his table, he was a king summoning a commoner. Half the people in the bar were watching these two men.

When Fargo reached Crowley's table, he said, "I figured you'd be wearing a crown."

The old man had a hearty laugh. "You've heard about me, huh?"

"Only from the desk clerk. I think he thinks you're the Pope."

"Well, you'd better not try to kiss my ring."

"I get to sit down or do I have to stand in your magnificent presence?"

"You're a smartass."

"So are you."

And with that, Crowley, who close up looked like a painting of someone who'd lived his life getting what he wanted, shoved a chair with his foot. The chair stopped at Fargo's thigh. Fargo sat down.

"You sit back here and they make a line passing by you and bowing, do they?"

"You always work this hard at being a prick, Mr. Fargo?"

"I guess I'm not much at bowing and scraping."

"Nobody asked you to bow and scrape."

"Not yet they haven't."

The waiter came and took their orders. Both men were drinking beer.

When the waiter had gone away, Crowley reached in the pocket of his suit coat and brought out a lumpy roll of greenbacks. "What would you say if I gave you all this money?"

Fargo shrugged. "I'm not all that interested in money."

"Why not? It's the only way we have to measure our success—or failure—while we're down here on earth."

"You have to work with too many bastards to make any big money."

"And I'm one of those nasty bastards?"

"I expect you are."

"How about if I told you that what I want you to do is help me change my reputation?"

The waiter returned with their schooners of beer and went away quickly.

"I'm assuming you asked around about me," Fargo said.

"Most definitely."

"Then you know that I've got a big problem right now with my memory."

"Your memory doesn't matter. What I want you to do is find out who shot you and killed Amy and the soldiers."

"You knew Amy?"

Crowley smiled. "We met at a regional banking convention once. She showed me a most pleasant time."

Fargo almost laughed out loud. He couldn't remember Amy, couldn't remember his feelings for her, and yet hearing that this man had slept with her made him jealous.

"We were rivals in the stagecoach business but we stayed friends," the patriarch went on. "I've already heard talk about how I was behind that robbery that got her killed. I don't play that way. Don't need to—I'm too rich already—and wouldn't even if I had to. I'm a son of a bitch to do

65

business with but I'm honest. I was trying to get some of her business and I'd be the first to admit it but I sure as hell wouldn't set with any robbery or getting anybody killed."

Then he said something that shocked Fargo. "I had an employee named Pat Nealon. He was my number-three man and he wanted to move up. He decided he was going to surprise me by eliminating Amy's business. He was the one who dressed up like an Indian and cut the reins of Amy's coach. He even hired a friend of his to kill her. But those robbers took care of that. He's also the one who tried to kill you. Nealon was afraid you'd get in the way of him wiping out Amy's business."

"How'd you find all this out?"

"He was a bad drunk was how I found it out. He told one of my men what he'd done and the man told me. I went looking for Nealon. He was with his killer friend. Nealon drew on me and I killed him. His friend drew on me, too, but he was so drunk he dropped his gun. But it was too late. I'd already fired when that happened. He died right then and there."

Fargo just stared at him. "All this worked out pretty well for you. A lot of people might've thought that you had Nealon cut those reins and try to kill me."

Crowley smiled coldly. "I let everybody insult me once. I put it up to ignorance. They don't know an honest man when they see one. And I'm an honest man. A ruthless man, true, but an honest one. Everything happened just the way I told you it did. If you want to push it any farther, Mr. Fargo, we have a big problem."

Fargo shrugged. "I'll take your word for it. For now, anyway."

A genuine laugh. "You're as much of an SOB as I am."

Fargo laughed in return. "I work at it as hard as I can, anyway."

Crowley raised his hand. Three people scuttled to deliver a fresh round to them. "I want to hire you. I need your help in clearing my son's name."

"Clearing it about what?"

"That robbery. And Amy's murder."

"People think he might be involved?"

"I'll be blunt with you. He has a reputation. He's been

in and out of trouble since he was twelve. The hell of it is, I didn't discourage him. I've got an older boy, too. Roger. I didn't want Nick to turn out like Roger."

"What's wrong with Roger?"

"He was sickly as a boy. His mother doted on him. He turned out—well, he's not a nancy or anything like that. But he's not very manly. He likes women well enough but that's about the only way you'd know he's got a pair of testicles on him. He runs my businesses, I'll give him that. He'll be taking over when I pass. He can tell you every nail, every board, every scrap of metal my various businesses own. But he doesn't give me the kind of pleasure Nick does. Nick's wild. He's always got three girls on the string and a few bruises from fistfights he gets into when he drinks too much. But he's my boy. He grew up being my favorite friend to go hunting or play blackjack or ride fence with. He's made a lot of enemies. I won't lie to you there. And a lot of them are right. He's handsome, he's big, he can have an ugly temper and he throws my name around a hell of a lot more than he should. But I love him and I don't want anybody trying to hang this robbery on him."

"What about the sheriff here? Can't he help you?"

"He's one of them that'd like to hang it on Nick. My son isn't exactly respectful of men who wear badges."

Fargo was impressed with Crowley. He could see why the man was successful. There was some brag there, true. But there was also an openness Fargo hadn't expected. He saw now that Crowley hadn't been bragging about sleeping with Amy. He'd simply been telling Fargo the truth about the whole situation.

"I'm not a detective, Crowley."

"Not an official one. But you've done some good work in that line. And you have a stake in this, Fargo. You want your memory back and I want my name cleared. I'm pretty sure that once you start working on this you won't stop until you find out what we both need to know."

"And if I don't?"

"Then you don't. You've got two docs saying that they believe you have amnesia. That's good enough for me. I believe you. So I'm showing faith in your story. Show a

67

little faith in mine. We both have good reasons to find out who killed Amy and took the money." He pushed the wad of bills across the table. "Five hundred dollars there. More if you find out what we need to know."

Crowley stood up. He obviously had a good sense of how impressive he was. He picked up a white hat and set it at a jaunty angle on his head.

"Buy yourself a good meal tonight," he said. Then, just as he turned to leave, "And get to work right away tomorrow morning."

Yes, sir, boss, Fargo thought.

You couldn't help but be impressed with the man.

You also couldn't help finding him a giant pain in the ass.

21

There were days when Roger Crowley didn't think about it at all.

Then there were days when it was difficult to think of anything else.

It was funny how a simple little meeting—in this case a meeting between himself and one of his former maids—could totally change one's life.

He wished he could take a knife and find the part of his brain where the terrible secret lay, and just cut it out.

Even if he confronted his beautiful, elegant wife Amanda about it, she would deny it—deny that the real father of their three-year-old daughter was Roger's younger brother, Nick.

He hadn't wanted to marry her anyway. She came from money and breeding—a Saint Louis debutante whose family moved out here when her father got into trouble for selling stock that was worthless—and never let him forget it.

At eighteen Roger had still been a virgin. He was a voracious romantic, even though his plain looks, sloppy posture and drab taste in suits led most women to believe otherwise. Even his parents thought of him that way. Nick would end up marrying somebody glittering and comely like Amanda. Roger would settle for one of the scrawny tomboys on one of the farms surrounding the town; or one of the dull shopgirls from town.

He'd always wondered why Amanda had shown such sudden interest in him. At the time Nick was courting a girl in the next county but scuttlebutt was that he was seeing Amanda Pekins on the sly.

Roger took his own lunch and ate in the park on warm days. He was too frugal—some would uncharitably use the word "cheap"—to eat at one of the cafés favored by the local businessmen.

One warm day he'd been eating and reading a week-old Saint Louis newspaper when a gentle voice said, "Do you suppose I could share your bench? All the other ones are full."

His mind returned to that day. So much of life was coincidence when you analyzed it. What if his bench had been filled that day? Or what if he'd said no? Or what if—even better—he'd not been in the park at all that day?

Six months later, they were married, Amanda insisting that she was pregnant with his child. His father ordered a wedding, bought them a fine, big house and gave an enormous party at the birth of his first and only grandchild.

A year later, Amanda fired their Norwegian maid Scoosh—Amanda could fire people faster than Roger could hire them, sometimes literally—and then, one day soon after, the woman stopped by his office in the new two-story redbrick building that was the headquarters of Crowley Enterprises, Inc., and nervously asked if she could see Vice President Roger.

He'd always liked the older, plain woman. When

Amanda was gone on one of her trips to see her sister in Saint Louis, Scoosh and he often played various card games, and at mealtime he invited her to dine with him. Amanda never took the child, so Roger had a chance to see how inept and indifferent a mother she was. Scoosh was the true nurturer, the true guardian of the little girl's body and soul.

In his office that day, Scoosh had said, "There's something I must tell you, Roger." He'd long ago given her permission to use his first name when they were alone. "You may resent me—even hate me—for telling you this. But the real father of your child is your brother Nick. I overheard your wife telling this to one of her friends one day. She said that she knew Nick would never marry her but that she could seduce you and make you think the baby was yours, but that she had to work very fast. She was seeing him on the side all the time she was seeing you. She got pregnant while you were gone to Denver for the month so she knew that it had to be Nick's."

If he hadn't loved little Simone so much, he would have confronted Amanda immediately. He knew he would someday confront her and then order her to leave his house. But every time he saw Simone of the soft blond hair and the even softer blue eyes . . . Roger had never loved anybody as much as he loved Simone.

The mayor was having a celebration party this morning. A company that manufactured hunting supplies had announced yesterday that it was moving here in two months.

There was a small gathering to honor the mayor's good work. The setting was outdoors; refreshments included ham, bread, cherry pie and coffee, nothing alcoholic. Birdsong brightened the laughing mood among the guests.

Urgent business kept Roger Crowley from dwelling anymore—for now—on the fact that his daughter wasn't his own.

The urgent business involved his only good friend in the entire town, the banker Karl Haskins. Or would, if Karl would show up. Haskins and his wife had definitely been invited. Where was he?

Amanda looked lost. She knew better than to look sullen

or bored. She liked to put on a good show for Martin Crowley.

Amanda looked lost for a simple reason. There was no one here to impress. She wore a new dress bought in Saint Louis that favored her long, lovely body. If there had been worthy men here she would have been making the rounds, making sure they all had a chance to compliment her.

But the males were mostly dull and uneducated men, to her, even though they were a wealth of stories, many of them true, about settling this land under the most difficult of circumstances.

Roger smiled to himself. He was glad there wasn't a proper audience for his wife to show off for.

But where the hell was Karl Haskins?

Then he was there, rushing in with his wife Ellen, a sweet, plain woman who bored Karl as much as Roger bored Amanda.

Karl and Ellen paid their respects to Old Man Crowley and then separated to greet others. Karl came straight to Roger. "Let's go for a little walk," he said.

"I was starting to wonder if you were ever going to show up."

They walked away from the party, to the open field where youngsters played baseball.

Karl and Nick had been friendly until four years ago, when Nick, good ole Nick, slept with the girl Karl—and the entire valley—assumed he would take for a wife. Nick seemed to be in some kind of contest to see how many lives he could ruin. The aftermath had been an embarrassing scene in Tully's Tavern the night the girl confided the truth to Karl. Karl drank twice as much as he ever had, swiped a Colt belonging to his brother, and went to Tully's and challenged Nick to a fight. Nick could have just relieved Karl of his gun, but he enjoyed humiliating people too much for that. He took Karl's gun, all right. But then he beat Karl so badly that Karl couldn't get out of bed for two full weeks. The girl he'd been seeing had been very pretty. So when Karl finally did take a bride, he took a plain one. He was like his friend Roger in that sense. Women were inscrutable and dangerous animals to them. A cougar could kill you but that was all it could do. A woman could betray you and put you in hell. In that sense,

71

the cougar was a merciful animal. Neither man had taken the trouble to learn that most women are fine, decent people.

Karl said, "Clemmons asked me some questions about the new quarterly profit and loss statement. I think he knows something's wrong. And you've got your audit coming up."

"You think I don't know that?" Roger snapped.

"I told you we never should've done it."

"Just once I wanted to do something on my own," Roger lamented. "Something that would buy my way out of here. Go to California. Start over. And then it goes off in my face."

"You were so damned sure you could find where Nick kept the money. I kept telling you how risky it was."

This was a new role for Roger Crowley and he didn't like it. To be the fool, to be the reckless one. His only virtues, at least as most others saw them, were those of common sense and good judgment.

Roger had been at the old man's place weeks earlier when a drunken Nick was sitting in the gazebo with Allie and Sievers. He'd heard all about the robbery and how much money they'd taken. Roger knew then and there how he would get out of the dilemma he'd let Karl make for both of them.

Karl was as dissatisfied with his predictable life as Roger was his. They both wanted to leave town. Karl was a banker who often received tips from clients on stocks worth investing in. Karl had told Roger about a mining stock that was, in the words of Karl's client, "going to make everybody rich." And to that end they'd each embezzled the money they needed to become investors.

It had all gone to hell. And quickly.

Oh, they'd bought the stock, but the great promise of the initial strike thinned out just two weeks in. The company kept telling its investors via telegram that they were sure this was only a momentary setback. No one believed it, of course. There'd been too many strikes like this to be naive about such matters.

The trouble was, they were both facing audits very soon and their embezzlements would be exposed. Their only chance of beating the audits was to find where Nick had hidden the loot.

"We need to work fast here," Karl said.

"Gosh, Karl, thanks for reminding me of that. I wouldn't have known that otherwise." Then, remarkably, Roger laughed. "You know who that sounded like?"

"Yeah. Your asshole brother, Nick."

Roger laughed again. Both of them heard the anxiety in the sound of it. "Maybe I'm turning into my brother."

"Oh, that's good news," Karl said. "That's just real good news."

But maybe this was a good thing, Roger thought. Roger wasn't tough. But Nick sure was. And if there was ever a time he needed the sheer ruthlessness of Nick, it was now.

Ruthless to the point, if need be, of killing somebody.

22

Her name was Mae Reynolds. She was twenty-one and had worked at the Royale Hotel since she was seventeen. She looked fine and fresh in her gingham dress. She looked even finer and fresher out of her gingham dress.

She stood completely naked now in the evening-shadowed room, displaying herself for his approval. He'd met her this morning when she'd been cleaning the hall. A look had passed between them far more articulate than words could ever be. The look said no time now, soon, soon.

Fargo, who was likewise naked, lay flat on the bed with his manly spear sticking straight up, hard and proud. The sight of those magnificent and bountiful breasts that swayed ever so slightly each time she moved had mesmerized him. She had huge pink nipples, ripe for teasing with the tongue and then kissing with full and tender passion.

Flaring hips, a perfect grotto of tightly curled blond hair between her legs, and thighs both tight and sumptuously white only made him stiffer.

"How about I ride you first and then you ride me?" she asked.

"No complaints here."

Moments later she was straddling him and taking his steely rod into her already moist treasure. She gasped in a mixture of pain and pleasure as his spear found its true home. "I'm not used to men your size."

"Well, we'll just have to do something about that, won't we?"

He took her hips in his hands and raised her so that she could ease in and out of him a few times until she was good and juicy and there was no pain.

And then it started. A furious ride that brought them both to a feeling of blinding need that bordered on insanity, their breathing coming in deathlike gasps that they each took turns laughing about. The weather might be cool autumn outside, but in room 263 of the Royale Hotel the heat was enough to make the weak faint.

Neither of these specimens was weak.

They threw themselves at each other with such force that the bed shuddered so much that they both wondered if it could collapse. He held her buttocks in such a tight grip that her juices spread all the way to her backside. The tone of her cries changed abruptly and he knew he had to help her to her ultimate satisfaction. And when it came she was as wild an animal as he'd ever bedded, jerking right and left in spasms that he sustained by jamming upward harder and harder.

And the moment she reached her true pleasure, he reversed positions, never pulling out of her, just starting to ride her so hard that her joy would continue to burst forth in reckless rushes that left them both unable to speak or even move for long minutes after they had managed to finish together.

"Oh, my Lord."

"What?"

"I think you spoiled me for any other man I'll ever sleep with."

He'd asked her this before, but now, after the passion had waned, it seemed sensible to ask her again. "Your boss doesn't mind if you fraternize with the guests?"

"He doesn't have to know."

"We made some noise."

"The only guests we've got right now are on the first floor. And to be honest, I would've done it anyway. I got a look at you naked when I was making up your bathwater this morning. You looked mighty fine to me, mister."

"Likewise," Fargo said.

He rolled over, snatched the makings from the chair next to the bed and rolled himself a smoke.

"I get some of that?"

"You smoke, huh?"

"I know ladies ain't supposed to smoke." She laughed. "But who said anything about me bein' a lady, huh?"

After passing the cigarette back and forth, her head now on his chest, he asked, "Do you know Nick Crowley?"

"Oh, you bet I do."

"Don't you like him?"

"You mean aside from the fact that he gave me a black eye one time and another time he nearly raped me? Why wouldn't I like him?"

"One of your favorites, huh?"

"Sure. Who doesn't like spoiled brats who think they can do anything they want and get away with it?"

"What about his brother?"

"Roger? Very nice man. Quiet, polite, shy. People make fun of him but I think he's a good man."

After a time, she sighed and said, "Well, I should get back to work." But then she eyed his hips and said, "Is that what I think it is standin' up down there?"

"Sure looks like it to me."

"Hmmm."

Then she went down there to find out for herself.

23

The café where he took his meal that night was so crowded Fargo had to wait half an hour to get inside. In the meantime, he sat on a bench in the front of the place smoking cigarettes and reading a couple of Territory newspapers.

When he got himself seated, he ordered coffee, Swiss steak, boiled potatoes, corn and a piece of pumpkin pie. The food was so slow in coming—but worth the wait—that he downed two cups of coffee before the tomato-covered steak was set down on his table.

When he reached across the table to grab the salt and pepper, he felt eyes on him and, when he glanced up, he saw her.

Young, pretty, dark-haired, she sat alone at a table to his right. Was it the same woman he caught staring at him on the street when he first arrived in town? He couldn't be sure, but he had the feeling it probably was.

A vague memory of her. Vague but pronounced enough that it troubled him. It was like trying to reach across a chasm that your fingers couldn't quite touch no matter how hard you strained.

But then the waitress was there and he had to look away from the young woman.

While he asked for another cup of coffee he saw, peripherally, the dark-haired woman stand up and make ready to leave her table and the crowded café in a hurry.

"Cancel that coffee," he said to the waitress. "You see that dark-haired woman over there?"

"Sure. That's Allie Blaine."

"Thank you."

The waitress smiled at him. "She's available, if that's what you want to know. She finally gave up on having Nick Crowley all to her own." She winked at him. "I doubt anybody ever will."

Praise the Lord for gabby waitresses. Some of them barely spoke to you. But there was a handful who would yammer and gossip all day.

But he'd paid a price for getting his information.

Allie Blaine was gone.

Fargo slapped money in the waitress's palm and said, "Pay what I owe and keep the rest."

"Thanks, mister." Then she winked again. "I'd say she's worth goin' after. Cute little thing."

He worked his way through the crowd of people at the front waiting to be seated. Then he was pushing through the front door and standing on the boardwalk, scanning left and right for any sign of Allie. None.

The memory of her again. Where had he seen her before? What part had she played in his unremembered life? Damn, it was frustrating. The robbery—Amy's death—had she played some part in those things? A sweet-faced young woman like that?

He decided to walk west, toward the raucous clamor of the saloons. She wouldn't be in any of them, of course. No women allowed except the drink-pushing dance girls.

He heard her before he saw her.

There was an alley a quarter block down. A horse was coming to its mouth. Coming a lot faster than it normally would in an alley.

Fargo drew his Colt and ran to the narrow, shadowy space between the buildings. He was just in time to see her. When she saw him, she started to lash the horse into a run, but Fargo said, "Stop."

In the shattered fragments of moonlight, he saw the fear and anger in her brown eyes. She was trying to decide, in a split second, whether she should ride on or stop. She decided, and reined in her horse. She obviously didn't know enough about the man to risk running away. She'd known her share of bad ones in her life—even a few who just might shoot a girl in the back if they felt it was necessary.

"Now get down from there nice and easy and ground-tie your animal. Then we'll have ourselves a little talk."

"I don't know who you think you are, mister."

"Shut up and get down from there."

"I wonder how you'd do against a man your own size instead of a poor, defenseless girl."

Fargo laughed. "I doubt you're a poor, defenseless girl. Now jump down, and I mean right now."

"Yes, sir, Commander, sir."

Fargo saw her eyes flash at a point somewhere behind him. But it was too late—way too late.

Allie Blaine laughed. That was the last thing he would remember before the explosion at the back of his skull, somebody hitting him awful hard with the barrel of an awful big gun.

He thought he heard her say, "You hit him too hard, Nick."

But he couldn't be sure.

And then there was nothing, just nothing at all.

24

Karl Haskins usually felt a little better after he beat his wife. He never beat her that hard, and he never beat her that long. But when a man had a lot of frustrations, he had to take them out on somebody, didn't he? And Karl Haskins had no illusions about himself as a fighter. To his shame his older sister Louisa had been able to beat the tar out of him till he turned sixteen. And even when she went and turned lady on him and no longer engaged in fisticuffs, he still held the secret dread that she could whip off her fancy hat and bustle and do him some serious damage with those tiny little fists of hers.

He sat alone in his parlor on this cold night, his mind unable to conceive of anything but a fate that would lead to prison. It had all looked so easy. He and Roger would take the money from the till, buy the stock with the money and then be rich in no time when the mine proved out— they'd be able to borrow against such a clear strain of gold.

He sucked on his knuckles. He'd bruised a knuckle smacking Ellen around. Normally that would mean that he'd temporarily unburdened himself of his demons.

Ellen had sullenly made him a good supper after the beating, and then went to their room and sulked. Damned women just couldn't take it the way men could. Well, except for his sister Louisa.

He'd seen Roger at the end of the day. Roger was coming apart. All their lives, Roger had been the calm one. Present him with a problem and he'd solve it efficiently, almost coldly, never expressing an emotion.

But now Roger was having the same nightmares that Karl was. Disgrace. Prison. Instead of the money the gold mine would give them, the money that would ultimately give them the freedom to slip quietly away from town here and start interesting new lives far away, all they had now was terror.

Roger was going to see his old man tonight and ask for a loan. Going to make up some excuse for needing money right away. An opportunity. Roger seemed to believe that his old man might actually come through for them.

But Karl knew better.

The only chance they had was to find the money Nick Crowley had stashed after the bank robbery.

His father was in the den, drinking Virginia whiskey, when Roger got there shortly after suppertime. The old man liked to have a huge fire going. He sat in his smoking jacket with his feet on a leather ottoman that matched the chair he sat in. He often sat with his feet up. He suffered frequently from gout.

Roger was too nervous to sit. His father always made him feel like a weak little boy, anyway. He said, "Cold."

The old man fixed him with those truth-seeking eyes and said, "You got something against that wing chair there?"

"No, sir."

"Good. Then sit in it."

"I'd rather stand up, Dad."

"What the hell are you so nervous about?"

"I'm not nervous, Dad. Shivering a little from the cold is all."

"Then stand nearer the fire."

"I guess that makes sense."

Roger was miserable already. The old man, as usual, was in total control of the situation. The funny thing was that there was probably no malice in the old man's suggestion. Roger knew that Nick was his father's favorite. But if nothing else the old man paid begrudging thanks for how well Roger oversaw his father's various businesses.

The old man would be devastated if he ever found out that Roger had embezzled money. The two qualities he'd always respected in his lesser son were intelligence and honor. He might prefer the swashbuckling tendencies of Nick. But he never depended on Nick the way he depended on Roger.

"You want some brandy?"

"No, thanks, Dad."

The old man smiled. "You ready to get to it?"

"Get to it? Get to what, Dad?"

"Get to the point. You sure as hell didn't come out here because I'm such interesting company. I have my qualities like anybody else, but I'm not much for small talk."

Roger took a deep breath. "I need a favor, Dad."

There. In one burst.

"All right, son. But I don't know why the hell you have to be so nervous about it. I do all I can for you." The old man, his hands folded in his lap, said, "If it's about a raise, I'll see to it right away. And the same for the annual bonus. I want to raise that by two percent. How's that sound?"

"I really appreciate that, Dad. But a raise—"

He gulped. Actually gulped. The old man's gaze got tighter, shrewder, as he tried to figure out what the hell was going on with Roger tonight.

"What I need is a loan."

Surprise shone in the old man's eyes. Roger was a saver; he kept tight rein on his expenses. His wife sometimes joked that Roger ran their home like an army camp. Every expenditure had to be cataloged and justified.

"Well, that shouldn't be any problem."

"It's a lot of money, Dad. What I need, I mean."

"Well, how much are we talking about?"

Roger gulped again. He felt his entire body tremble. He just kept imagining the auditor's report when he discovered that discrepancy.

"Nineteen thousand dollars, Dad."

The old man whistled. "Boy, Roger, when you want a loan you don't fool around." He put his head back against his wing chair. "Do I get to know what this is for?"

"An investment. A shipping company back east. I'm buying a part of it from a college friend of mine. He's had a falling-out with his partner and he wants me to buy the man out."

This was the lie he'd been rehearsing for the past three hours. He surprised himself. The lie came out polished, believable, comfortable.

It was the next lie that was going to give him trouble.

The old man said, "I get to see some documentation on this company? I assume you've got an overview on profit and loss, and what he thinks the potential is for investments."

"All that's on its way."

"You mean you haven't done any kind of due diligence?"

"Haven't had time, Dad. Been so busy at work and all. And this just came up. The third partner wants the share for himself. But that would leave him president of the company and leave my friend working for him. He wouldn't have much say in what happened anymore. He needs the money right away."

They were silent now with the noise of the wicked wind

rattling the windows, and the wood in the fire hissing and popping.

The old man said, "There's something you're not telling me, Roger."

"I'm not holding anything back, Dad. I promise."

The old man said, "Son, I'll admit we've never been real close. But that doesn't mean I'm not grateful for all you've done in running the family business. And it doesn't mean that I don't love you. But you've got me scared now, Roger. I've never seen you like this."

"Dad, listen—"

The old man shook his white-maned head. "Listen? Listen to what—more lies?" His face showed sudden but deep grief.

"Roger, I don't give a damn about the money. I've got that money in the safe right there on the west wall behind that painting of Washington. It's not the money—it's what's going on with you. I'm scared for you, son."

For a long moment, Roger was tempted to throw himself on the mercy of the court. That's what this situation was like. He was on trial.

But he couldn't. As much as he'd hated the old man at some points in his life for so obviously preferring Nick to him, he just couldn't bear seeing what the old man would look like if Roger told him.

The old man had the reputation of a ruthless businessman who usually ended up getting what he wanted. But his pride was that he was honest, and everybody acknowledged that.

But if the one son who shared his father's reputation for honesty was to reveal himself as an embezzler—

It happened so quickly, Roger was barely aware of doing it.

He was hurrying across the Persian rugs that covered the floors from the fireplace to the den door.

"Roger! Roger! Come back here, son!"

The plaintive notes—the notes of worry and fear and sorrow—haunted Roger all the way home.

25

There was darkness but there was pain, and in Fargo's state, the pain signified life. He wasn't dead.

The girl Allie. Approaching her. Drawing his gun. Somebody from behind. "Nick." And then darkness again.

One of his eyelids raised. Then the other.

Staring up into the face of an angel. Maybe he was dead. Fargo had always thought of angels as blond for some reason. This one was dark-haired, with classically elegant facial features and eyes so blue they were almost unearthly.

The smell of medicines. White walls. And the doctor, with a wooden stethoscope checking his heart rhythms now.

"I'd say you were going to live, Mr. Fargo. I'm Dr. Rena Adams, by the way."

"You can't be a doctor."

"Because I'm a woman?"

"Because you're so beautiful."

She smiled. "Beauty is in the eye of the beholder, Mr. Fargo. I'm reminded of that every time I remember that my fiancé back east threw me over when I told him I wanted to go to medical school. Every once in a while people tell me that I'm pretty but it still doesn't do much for me. I apparently wasn't pretty enough for him." She eased the cold cloth evenly across his forehead. It had started to slide off. "But you're the patient here, not me."

"This time I remember everything about getting attacked."

"Good. The sheriff stopped by and explained about your amnesia. I was interested to see if being knocked out the way you were tonight might bring back other memories."

"Afraid not." He winced from a stabbing pain on the side of his head. "I have a concussion?"

"A very mild one. You'd be better off staying here tonight. I sleep on a bed in the next room. I can look in on you every few hours, see how you're doing."

"That sounds nice."

"Don't get any ideas, Mr. Fargo. First of all, you're in no condition to be thinking about anything except resting. And second of all, I haven't been with a man since my fiancé bid me farewell. And I'm not in any rush to be, either. Even with a man as good-looking as you."

"You could always change your mind."

"Yes, I could. But I won't. Now I'm going to turn down that oil lamp over there and I'd strongly urge you to rest."

He patted the cot she'd put him on. "Where's my Colt?"

"In the examination room. I don't think you'll be needing it."

"I'd appreciate it if you'd go get it and set it right next to me."

"In your condition?"

"Wait a minute. You're saying my concussion isn't bad, but you don't think I can have sex and now you don't think I should have my Colt? You're confusing me."

"You're not in the best of condition is all I'm saying. I'm not challenging your masculinity, Mr. Fargo."

He smiled. "Well, thanks for that, anyway."

She walked away from his cot. She was a tall, slender woman in a white medical jacket of the type you saw frequently in Eastern magazines. Her beauty was absolutely heartbreaking. He assumed that her fiancé was in an insane asylum back east somewhere.

She turned in the doorway. "You think they'll come after you?"

"Who's 'they'?"

"Well, whoever did you in tonight."

"It's a possibility."

"Then I'd better get my Remington."

"You have a gun?"

"Believe it or not, yes. The medical school I went to urged young women who were going west to learn how to shoot."

"You're one impressive lady."

For just a moment, that elegant face looked sad. "Too bad my fiancé didn't think so."

Nick and Allie found Hap Sievers in a card game—where else?—and dragged him out of it. Then the three rode over to Allie's little place.

Allie got a fire going and put some coffee on. They sat at her wobbly kitchen table.

"I hope this was worth it," Sievers said.

Nick Crowley glanced at Allie and winked. "Saved you from losing all your money, Hap."

"The hell? I was winning that hand."

"The first one you probably won all night," Allie teased.

"The second," Sievers said. "If you have to be so damned nosy."

"How many did you lose tonight?" Crowley said.

"Not that many."

"How many?" Allie asked.

"Ten, maybe."

"Maybe?" Allie said.

"Twenty, more like it." Crowley said this while rolling a smoke.

"Twelve, but I prob'ly would've won it all back," Sievers said.

"Sure you would've, Hap."

"And don't wink at her no more. That pisses me off." Then, "And since you're so damned smart about everything, where the hell's our money?"

"Safe and sound is where it is."

"You're prob'ly gonna run off with it."

Crowley sighed. "Hap, think about it. If I was going to run off with it, wouldn't I have done it by now?"

"Well, I think we got a right to know."

"So do I," Allie said.

"So I let you know. Then what?" Crowley leaned back in his chair. He took a deep drag of his cigarette. "I'm doing you a favor. If Hap here knew where I hid it, you don't think he'd go after it to pay off his gambling debts?" He spoke directly to Allie.

She shrugged. "I guess that's a possibility."

"And Hap, you know how bad Allie here wants to get out of this town, don't you? It's all she ever talks about. What if she knew where I hid the money? You don't think she'd be tempted to grab it and ride out of here?"

Sievers stared at Allie. "You do hate this town, Allie."

Allie said, "And I suppose you don't, Nick."

"I can't afford to ride out of here. People already suspect I had a hand in it. They'd slap a reward on my head and every bounty hunter in the Territory'd come looking for me." The reasoned, even tone of his speech surprised both Allie and Sievers. They'd never heard him like this— forthright, reassuring. He was usually snapping orders or belittling them somehow. "That's why I say I'm doing you a favor. The money's safe and as soon as it's clear, we'll divvy it up. But right now, we've got bigger problems, anyway."

"That Fargo bastard," Sievers said.

Crowley nodded. "One of us'll have to kill him."

"He claims he can't remember anything," Sievers said.

"He spotted me tonight," Allie said. Then she told him about Fargo staring at her in the café and coming after her. "Good thing Nick saw what was happening. Fargo's going to remember everything sooner or later."

"If I get the chance, I'll kill him," Nick said.

Sievers scoffed. "Big bad Nick."

Nick glared at Sievers. "You thought that woman Amy was dead. Good thing I saw she wasn't and killed her for you."

26

The dream was of bacon and eggs. And coffee.

While Fargo's dreams usually ran to bare-naked women or silver, babbling brooks where the fishing was unparalleled, this dream was definitely of more mundane origin—his grumbling, empty stomach.

And there was a reason for that. The good Dr. Rena Adams held a platter of three basted eggs, four slices of bacon and a large slab of jelly-slathered bread out to him.

"You think you can sit up?"

"That might be arranged."

"I checked on you three times last night—and every time I heard that stomach of yours growling."

He sat up. The headache stabbed at him once but then faded quickly.

"I wish I could solve all my problems this easily," she said, handing him the platter. A knife and fork lay crosswise on it.

He couldn't recall when he'd last been this hungry. "I'm told I make noise when I eat."

That lovely smile. "I've heard a lot worse noises in my time, Mr. Fargo."

As he began lustily destroying the food, she pulled up a stool and sat across from him. "So what's on your agenda for the day?"

"You're the doc old Grimes told me about. The pretty

one." Then, "What I'm going to do is hunt down the girl from the alley last night. The one named Allie."

"You sure it was her?"

"Positive."

The doctor shook her head. "She came here several times last spring."

"Sick?"

"Sick in the heart."

"Heart problems?"

"Love problems."

"Oh."

"Nick Crowley scored another broken heart."

He paused long enough to study her face. "Not a fan of Crowley's?"

"I like the old man and the other son, Roger, very much. They helped me get established when I came here. A lot of people didn't want a woman doctor here. The women thought I'd seduce all their men and the men thought I'd put a lot of foolish 'Eastern' notions in their wives' heads. But Roger and the old man made my case for me. They were my first two clients, in fact."

"Nick didn't come here?"

"Oh, he came here, all right. Late one night. Very drunk. Seems he thought I'd fall in love with him on the spot. Tried to get in and spend the night here. Said there were bad things he needed to protect me against." She smiled. "I told him that the only thing I needed protection from was him. I finally had to pull my Colt on him and chase him out."

"I bet he didn't like that."

"You have a piece of egg hanging off your chin."

"Bet it makes me look purty."

"Oh, yes. Very fetching." She shrugged. "Anyway, Nick's never bothered me again. I think he's still in shock that I pulled a gun on him. I wish little Allie had done the same thing. She didn't have much of an upbringing, you know. Practically had to raise herself. So I think Nick was both her lover and her father in some ways. She told me that if she had the money, she'd leave this town. I urged her to leave without any money. Go to a big city. A pretty girl like her could find work easily. But she said she wanted to do it right. Take a train to Chicago. Find a nice boarding-house. Maybe go back and get a little more education. Really make something of herself. And for that she'd need money, but what I couldn't figure out was where she was going to get that kind of money around here."

Bank robbery, Fargo thought. But he didn't say anything.

"How's the food? There're actually two more eggs and a few strips of bacon."

"You're not eating?"

"Already have. A big bowl of New England porridge, just the kind my mother used to make me every morning before school."

Fargo tapped his fingers against his stomach.

"Is that a new medical procedure?" the doctor asked.

"I'm just looking to see if there're any empty spots left in my stomach."

"Are there?"

He found a spot and tapped it three or four times. "Well, I'll be dogged."

"An empty spot, Mr. Fargo?"

"Hard to believe, isn't it?"

She laughed. "I'd have to say that you're doing much better this morning with that slight concussion you brought in here."

He handed her the empty platter. "The remarkable cura-tive powers of bacon and eggs," he said, sounding like one of those patent-medicine barkers who offered their magic elixirs out of the back end of a wagon.

"I hope you don't faint from starvation before I get back, Mr. Fargo."

He watched her, with profound appreciation, as her slen-der but shapely body went to fetch him more stomach-fillers.

27

Two hours later, Fargo walked up to Allie Blaine's small white house. The fall day was bright enough that he had to squint sometimes, his headache faint but still there. He had the feeling that eyes behind the front window curtains had been watching him for the past few minutes.

Now, when he heard the back door open and close, he was sure of it.

Behind the house was open land that gave way to timber after a few hundred yards. The timber would offer a whole lot of hiding places.

He hustled around the side of the house just in time to see Allie start walking quickly across the open field. Given his weakened condition, he wasn't up to giving chase for very long.

He drew his Colt and fired carefully. The bullet passed less than six inches from her head. She screamed, tripped on some gnarled earth and fell flat on her face.

"You try running again and I'll shoot you in the leg."

She was already getting up, dusting off the front of her denims and flannel shirt. "Big, brave man."

"Big, brave woman. Had to have good old Nick-boy sneak up on me and hit me across the head."

He was close enough to see the surprise on her face. He wasn't supposed to know that Nick Crowley had been involved last night.

"You have a complaint, go to the sheriff." She dusted her shirtfront with small but strong-looking hands.

"Sheriff can't help me. But you can."

"Oh? And just what can I help you with?"

"Tell me where the money is."

Surprise showed once again on her pert, freckled face. "What money?" she said after she'd composed herself.

"The army money you took a few weeks back. And killed three people in the process."

She watched him for a long moment. "They told me you didn't have much of a memory left. But they didn't tell me you were crazy, too."

"That's a good one. You must've worked on that awhile." He pointed the Colt at her and said, "Let's go back to the house."

"For what?"

"You're going to sit there and watch me look through everything."

"You are crazy. You won't find anything."

"Then all you have to do is sit there and watch me waste my time."

She was one of those knickknack collectors: tiny dolls, tiny religious figures, tiny figurines of everything from mountain men to George Washington and Thomas Jefferson. The furniture was old, dusty and badly battered. The small interior smelled of cooking, and not good cooking at that. Scorched. Maybe the next time she paid a visit to Dr. Rena Adams, she could ask the good doctor to give her cooking lessons.

When he knelt down to look under her single bed, she laughed. "You're getting old, Fargo. Listen to those bones crack."

He was smart enough not to answer. He ended his search by looking through the cupboards. He found nothing. "You tell good old Nick for me that this is just the beginning."

"Good old Nick just might not like you much."

"I'll probably survive."

"I wouldn't bet on it, Fargo. Good old Nick, as you call him, has got a terrible temper. Just about the worst temper I've ever seen, in fact."

He walked to the front door. "A good friend of mine got killed that night."

"So you hear. You don't remember, though, do you?"

"No. Not right now." He glared at her. "But when I do remember, good old Nick better have that temper of his good and ready."

She glared right back at him for a few seconds, but the rage in those lake blue eyes put goose bumps on her arms and suddenly she looked away.

Fargo was on his Ovaro stallion and headed toward the road that would take him back to town when he heard, around the bend several hundred yards away, the sounds of a horse coming toward him fast. Allie's being the only house for half a mile in either direction, the rider was no doubt going there.

Fargo hurried his horse into a stand of pine trees near the house. He tied the stallion to a low-hanging branch, felt his sinuses adapt to the assault of the pine odor and then hid behind two trees that verged on the grassy yard belonging to Allie.

He knew right away that this couldn't be Nick Crowley. This man was older, wore worn work clothes and looked a lot more agitated than an arrogant young man like Crowley would. There wasn't a hint of swagger as he headed toward the house.

Fargo's first thought, now that he'd gotten a look at the man, was to head back to town. But then he decided it would be better to find out who the man was. He'd follow him.

He didn't have to wait long. The man emerged from the house after only a few minutes. He appeared even more agitated than he had when he'd arrived.

Allie and the man stood outside talking for a few more minutes. The man got angry once and shouted something at her. The wind was strong enough that it tore all the words into unintelligible bits and pieces. Something was up, anyway. Could this man also have been involved in the robbery and killings?

The man didn't say good-bye from the saddle. He just eased his horse around and headed back to the road. Allie stood there in the thin autumn sunlight, nervously playing with a button on her flannel shirt. Now she looked as agitated as her visitor had.

She stood there a moment longer, shaking her head as if in misery, then she turned and went back inside.

Fargo had no trouble picking up the trail of the stranger. The man stayed on the road, and he rode at a lope. Fargo had to stay far behind. The road was narrow and lined on both sides with pines. The man would have no trouble hearing Fargo's horse if he got too close. Hoofbeats would be pronounced in these confines.

Near the town limits sign, the man stopped at what looked to be a railroad shanty but was in fact a house built of scrap materials. There was a new tin chimney on it and what appeared to be a relatively new, adobe-covered well casing.

The man dismounted and went inside.

This time, Fargo ground-tied his stallion and crept up to the outhouse close to the shanty. He had the same problem again. He could hear talk—shouting, actually—a man and a woman and then a baby squalling, but the wind robbed the meaning of the sounds.

The man didn't stay long here, either. A thin woman holding a small baby stood in the doorway watching him go. She rocked the baby, all the time sobbing loudly. She needed to be held and rocked, too. The man showed no sympathy, just anger as he pointed his horse back toward town and took off at a gallop.

In town it was more difficult to follow him, but Fargo got lucky after a block and was able to partially hide behind a large, rumbling wagon. The man he followed had shown no sign that he knew somebody was tailing him.

The man took an alley. Fargo now had to hurry. But he had to be careful, too. He quickly tied his Ovaro to a hitching post and hurried into the alley in time to see the man direct his horse to an open area where a buggy and two other horses were being kept away from alley traffic.

The man rushed to a back door and went inside. Even before he got the door closed, he was saying, "Sorry I'm late getting back here, Mr. Tate."

The door was slammed shut.

Fargo waited a minute and then strolled down to the place the man had disappeared into. He didn't want to give anybody the impression that he had any special interest in the alley. He was just out for a walk.

The door had a small sign on it:

TATE'S BUTCHER SHOP
PLEASE USE FRONT DOOR

Tubs of raw meat and gristle and fat were lined up in a row. Stuff so rotten that not even the most larcenous butcher would try to pass it off as edible. Not that the condition of the meat discouraged the flies. Entrails had turned this into a bloody holiday for them.

The stench started to overwhelm him.

28

His brother, Roger, said, "I need some of that robbery money of yours."

Nick Crowley stared in disbelief at the sight of his timid older brother, Roger. For one thing, how the hell had Roger managed to get into Nick's rented room? For another, since when had Roger started packing a six-shooter? And most of all, how had Roger found out about the robbery?

Nick's hand dropped automatically to his own weapon but Roger said, and not without visible joy, "Right now I wouldn't mind killing you, you bastard. And I'll do it, too, if you try and pull your gun. Pitch it on the bed over there."

Nick did as he was told but immediately tried to effect control of the situation. He gave his brother his best big, handsome grin, like somebody holding a gun on him didn't faze him at all, and said, "You know, big brother, our old man would laugh if he ever heard you were packin' a gun."

"Sit down on that chair over there and shut up."

The disbelief hadn't left Nick. This was like waking up and finding yourself in a different world.

But sit down he did. And shut up he did.

"I embezzled some money from the old man to invest in a stock."

This time Nick's big handsome cowpoke grin was real. "You? Perfect little Roger? You embezzled some of the old man's money?"

"Yes, I did. And it was the dumbest thing I ever did in my life. I don't know what the hell I was thinking of."

This was the strangest and most intimate conversation the two brothers had ever had. And it made both of them damned uncomfortable.

"And now I need to pay it back. There's a bank audit next week."

"Looks like you got your balls in a vise."

"Thanks for pointing that out." The tone was droll. Big coward brother being droll?

"Damn. You got any other secrets you want to tell me about, Roger? You been whorin' around? You been goin' downriver and gettin' in gunfights, Roger?"

"I need one-third of that bank robbery money."

Nick gave up his pose of nonchalance. "I don't know what the hell you're talking about, Roger, so you might as well get the hell out of here. You came to the wrong place and the wrong man."

Roger reached inside his suit coat and yanked out a green military bag that tied at the top. The kind of bag the army shipped money in. He tossed it over to Nick.

Nick caught it. "What's this supposed to mean?"

"It means I found it in the bottom drawer of your bureau over there. Bad idea to keep things like that around."

"This doesn't prove anything."

"Not in a court of law, maybe. But if I took it to the sheriff he'd be damned interested."

"You son of a bitch. You're trying to blackmail me, aren't you?"

Roger smiled coldly. "If that's what you want to call it. Personally, I see it more like reparations for all the times you beat me up and made fun of me and took anything of mine you wanted. Big bad Nick. The men are scared of him and the ladies want him in their beds." Rage was on him now, a lifetime of rage turning his voice bitter. "But it had to end someday, Nick. Your luck couldn't hold forever. You talk too much when you're drunk. I heard you talking to Allie and Sievers about the robbery." The cold smile again. "And as things turned out, I need some of that money for myself."

"You think I won't tell the old man about you embezzling?"

"You never were too bright, Nick. Think it through. You tell the old man about my embezzling. And then I tell him about your robbery—and the three people you killed."

"That was that stupid asshole Sievers."

"Yeah? Well, if he's so stupid why did you hire him?"

In just a few minutes Nick's pose of arrogance had degenerated into sour misery. He started shaking his head back and forth. He'd planned all along on grabbing the money and leaving Allie and Sievers holding an empty bag. But now there was a new and even more dangerous factor involved—his milquetoast brother. Who, it seemed, was not at all as milquetoast as Nick had figured.

"I'm as desperate as you are, Nick. You better keep that in mind. If I don't get a share of that money—and I mean by tomorrow morning—no telling what I'll do. And that includes going to the sheriff."

Nick tried to sneer but he suddenly felt too exhausted to start posing again. "You can't. The old man'd find out you embezzled."

"True enough. But again, Nick, which is worse? Embezzling, or robbing the federal government and then killing three people? I'd get two or three years in prison. That is, if the old man decided to press charges. But you'd get hanged, Nick. They'd bring you to trial so fast you wouldn't even have time to find some shyster lawyer to come up with a good story for you. These are the *federales*, Nick. And they want vengeance."

Nick covered his face with his hands. He used to do this when the old man caught him doing something he wasn't supposed to. With big hands over his face, Nick could gift himself with the notion that he had willed all bad things out of existence. But it never lasted long.

He heard Roger stand up. "You'd better get rid of that money bag, Nick. It's crazy to keep it around. Just like it'd be crazy not to have that money for me tomorrow morning."

The formerly timid older brother of Nick Crowley then strode, with great calm, out the door.

29

Fargo spent the afternoon hours reading through old editions of the local newspapers, seeing if the names Nick Crowley, Allie Blaine or Hap Sievers appeared. Only Sievers appeared—an arrest for drunk and disorderly.

He got far more information from the librarian. He told her about his amnesia and said he was just trying to piece his life back together. She was sympathetic. She also looked lonely.

"Well, Hap Sievers, he's quite the town legend actually—and not in a good way."

There was at least one Sievers in every town, big or small, in the West.

He had one particularly nasty vice he'd never been able to overcome. He played poker. If there was a worse player in the Dakota Territory, he had yet to come forward. Most of the local players refused to sit at a table with him. None of the local saloons or men's clubs would allow him to be seated, because he brought new meaning to the term "bad sport."

When he played, he lost, and when he lost, he drank, and when he drank, he got openly morose about what a shitty father and husband he was to be sitting here spending his family's payday money like this. And when he got morose, he got violent. And when he got violent, God forbid you were the particular player who'd taken the biggest share of his money from him that night.

Because then the head-kicker and bone-smasher waited outside for you. He never tried to take his money back. He just wanted you to pay a bloody price for beating him at the table and thus turning him into an even worse father-husband-provider. Somehow he never saw himself as the problem; he saw you as the problem.

He kept on gambling, of course. There was always a game in some alley or back room or cellar. Maybe the place smelled of rats; maybe there was a latrine less than five feet from the place; maybe it was a root cellar setup that smelled of the very same cold earth everybody was eventually buried in.

It didn't matter. Because he got to play.

All of this was interesting to Fargo because he was getting a picture of a man who was constantly in debt. In fact, another thing he learned about Sievers was that he owed just about every merchant in town. No more credit for the Sievers family. And for this reason he took the back way to and from work, the empty grassy plain that nobody used much. He didn't want to see his creditors.

Sounded like a man who could use a bank robbery to get him out of a jam.

30

The smallest of Hap Sievers's six children was coughing so hard in his sleep that Sievers wondered if the little one was coming down with whooping cough.

Two of Sievers's older brothers had died of that back when he was a little boy. Whooping cough was his bogey-man. Just the mention of it sheened his body with a cold sweat. Hell, he even had nightmares about it.

He sat in the darkness of his small home. The air was smoky from the potbellied stove, and warm from the body heat that his wife and six young ones produced in their sleep.

He kept thinking about that Fargo character. He was one determined son of a bitch, that was for sure.

He listened to the kids snore and was momentarily touched by the sounds they made. He was pretty rough on them sometimes—he probably didn't have to beat them quite so hard when he was chastising them—but they were a burden. He could probably concentrate a lot better on his poker hands if he didn't have to take the welfare of his kids into consideration. Being the kind of good father he was wasn't easy. He had to make sacrifices.

His family had no idea the kinds of sacrifices he made for them.

He wished he hadn't taken off his boots.

Now he'd have to be very quiet and crawl around looking

for them in the darkness. He sure couldn't light a candle or turn up the oil lamp.

A couple times he froze in his search, fearing that he'd awakened somebody.

And wouldn't there be hell to pay if she caught him sneaking out the door?

But finally boots were on feet, winter coat in place, six-shooter stuffed down the front of his jeans. And he was sneaking out the door.

The night was much colder than he'd anticipated.

Frost and moonlight sheened the summer-burned grass a coarse silver, like the skin of some exotic animal.

He wasn't sure where he was going or who he was going to talk to. But a sensible starting place was a saloon, wasn't it? A man could sit and drink or talk. A saloon was an excellent place to expand on your greatest whiskey thoughts. And not even wifey could object, could she?

He was as excited as he usually was about sex. Maybe even more so.

All that robbery money, his debts paid, and then his luck would change for sure and he'd need a wheelbarrow to carry his winnings home from the card tables. And no more alleys and basements and barns. He'd be invited back to the best places in town. A respectable gent.

He was so lost in these merry fantasies that he didn't notice the man who had divided from nightshadow and was now following him.

31

Finally, Allie couldn't hold it any more.

She'd been hiding behind the shed out behind the rooming house where Nick Crowley was presently living. She had decided that the money would be hers, not Nick's, not Sievers's. She'd been of the mind that there should be no more killing. But by this time she had no doubt that one or both of them would kill her and take her money.

So she would surprise both of them.

She would start following Nick at various times. Eventually, he'd lead her to where he'd hidden the money. Eventually, she'd kill him and take it for her own.

But first there was a little problem with her bladder.

Had to pee. Just had to.

She'd been sitting out in the autumn night, watching silver frost accumulate on the surface of just about everything. The cold, even with gloves and a heavy winter jacket, was bad enough. Nose frozen, hands numb and bladder about to explode.

She'd have to squat down right here and do it, and freeze her pretty little bottom off when she slid out of her butternuts.

But what choice was there?

She did the deed. The stream she made was noisy on the brittle autumn leaves. The horses, which must've had damned good ears, stirred in their sleep, apparently responding to the clatter of urine on leaves.

As she finished up, she looked at the cold prairie stars. In the summer the stars were romantic. But in the colder months she always felt their distance and their indifference. She had the sense that her pastor would strongly disapprove of such thoughts. He would say that the answers to all could be found in the Bible, not in contemplating the stars, wondering about their meaning, which human beings shouldn't be doing, anyway. It wasn't any business of mortals.

While she was jerking her butternuts up, she heard the back door slam. Nick. Had to be. The rest of the residents in the boardinghouse were old men. But Nick—she was right in waiting for him here. Too early for him to turn in. Nick usually went to sleep only when he was ready to pass out from all the liquor. And that was usually late at night.

She had ground-tied her horse down the alley. Now she separated from her shadow self behind the shed and ran down to her mount.

Tonight she'd have her money.

She was sure of it.

An hour after Allie began following Nick Crowley, Sheriff Cordell looked down at the body of Hap Sievers and said, "Hold that lantern closer. I want a better look at him."

"Just like in them books you read, huh, Sheriff?"

His night deputy was named Monk Young. If you made out a list of things to do each night, Monk would do them dutifully. In that respect he was a pretty good man for the nighttime. He was big enough to stop most brawlers. He was friendly enough to please the respectable citizens of town. And if he didn't bathe every week, he at least bathed every other week. He understood action. What he didn't understand was most things that involved thinking. Sheriff Cordell made a point of reading actual books on modern law enforcement. This didn't make Monk mad, it just baffled him. A feller could be playin' cards, visitin' one of the cribs where all the gals would give a man with a badge a discount on their services, sittin' around and exchanging thigh-slappers with some other drunks, or just sleeping. But why would you waste your time reading a book—or, for that matter, a magazine or even a newspaper? Monk just didn't get it.

He lowered the lantern.

Cordell got down on his knees and gave Sievers a long examination. The two shots had been fired from behind him. They had exited via his forehead. Cordell would get the body over to the undertaker's so the widow wouldn't have to see her husband. He would, in fact, tell her, "For your own sake, Jessie, be better if you didn't see him."

"He sure looks dead, don't he, Sheriff?"

"Dead people usually do look dead, Monk."

"Not all of them. One night I seen a feller—"

"Okay, Monk. I'll take your word for it." He stood up. "Get on your horse and ride to the undertaker and tell him we need his wagon back here pronto."

"You know how cranky he gets."

"Why would I give a damn about how cranky he gets? It's his job. And he makes a damn good living at it, believe me. The town council keeps any other undertakers from coming in here and cutting into his business. So you don't worry about what time it is."

"Yes, sir," Monk said, knowing that he'd just been reprimanded. Sometimes you couldn't be sure with Cordell. Other people, when they reprimanded you, they yelled or jabbed you in the chest or even gave you a little shove. But Cordell never yelled; he just put this real pissy edge on his voice.

"And tell him to get his ass in gear."

"Yes, sir, you bet."

While he waited, shivering beneath the too-light jacket he wore, Cordell got his pipe lighted good and steady, and then walked around the open ground in back of the lumber store. One thing his law enforcement books always insisted on was what they called "sweeping the crime area." In this case, it meant taking that lantern and going over the entire area around the corpse, looking for some clue that would identify the killer. Could be as small as funny-shaped boot tracks; could be as obvious as a ring dropped and overlooked as the killer ran quickly away.

He didn't find any odd boot tracks or any ring. He found something even more interesting. He found a piece of Navajo turquoise that looked as if it had been on some kind of jewelry. Since it was the only thing he found of even remote interest, he congratulated himself on being a very clever and modern detective.

He had just slipped the stone piece in his jacket pocket when the undertaker's wagon came bumping and rolling along the stage road next to the grassy field.

32

"I'm glad you got my note."

"I'm glad I got your note, too."

"You could always come inside, Skye," the young and piquant Dr. Adams said. Tonight she was dressed in a blue cotton blouse and a pair of black butternuts. Her hair was pulled back in a chignon. Fargo couldn't ever remember seeing a woman so delicately made. "In fact, I've got some apple cider simmering, too."

"Usually have mine with rum."

"I thought you might. So I bought some of that, too."

He followed her inside. A fire crackled in the fireplace, its colors playing across the tan-colored wallpaper and the dark furniture.

"Why don't we go into my office first?" Dr. Adams said. "I'd like to check your eyes."

"Is that what this is? I guess from your note I thought this was more of a social call."

"Why can't it be both? Now let's have a look at your eyes."

When she was finished with her examination, she parked Fargo in an easy chair by the fire and then went to get them rum-laced cider and some cookies she'd made.

"Have any luck finding Allie?" she asked when they both had food and drink, and she sat on the wide arm of Fargo's chair.

It was tempting to just slide his arm around her waist and pull her down to him. His crotch was beginning to fill his lap. "Found her. Didn't get what I wanted."

"You talk to Sheriff Cordell?"

"No, why?"

"He came here a few times asking me if I'd seen you. I didn't mention Allie or anything else."

"I appreciate that."

They sat silent for a time. The leaping flames seemed to contain ghosts for both of them. They stared at incidents from their pasts. Bad, hurtful incidents. They both carried hurts of all kinds with them all the time, hurts always ready to jump out at them like ghouls.

She could put names and places to hers, I'll bet, Fargo thought. I just see pictures. I'm not sure who I'm seeing or what we were even doing together. The funny thing was, even though he didn't know any of the specifics, he still felt the ache, knew somehow that these images were times of pain and loss for him.

But even as his mind dealt with these odd memories, his male needs continued to swell.

Done with his food and drink—and she had really loaded up on the rum—he set his cup down and did just what he'd been thinking about doing.

He slid his arm around her waist, turned her to face him and started to pull her down on his lap.

She laughed and tried to speak intelligibly. "I've got a mouthful of cookie."

"You don't think that's going to bother me, do you?"

He started undoing her blouse. She kissed him playfully with her mouthful of cookie. "Tastes good," Fargo said. "Give me a little bit more."

"You're crazy—you know that?"

By now, he'd slipped her blouse down to her hips. Her naked breasts were perfectly shaped, the sort you saw on

Roman statues of timeless beauties. Her skin was so taut yet tender that he felt an electricity shoot through his fingers and into his arm.

She ran her tongue around the edge of her lips. Fargo felt another erotic charge. "There. No more cookie."

She took his hand and led him to the rug before the hearth. The air was warm, the scent of the burning logs almost hypnotic.

They wasted no time.

Once they were both naked, he got his finger up her hot, wet sex and felt her hips begin to grind his. He let her work against his finger for a time, a prelude to what was soon to happen.

He slid his hand around behind her buttocks and lifted her up so he could bring her down on the hard lance of his cock. And then she really went to work, grasping his buttocks hard so she could grind his cock up deeper inside her. And then they found a heady, breathless rhythm that had them both panting and making little animal mewls of blinding pleasure.

He turned her over suddenly and took her from the back side. They were erotic silhouettes against the leaping flames. His lance drove deeper and deeper into her as her face began to slowly descend to the rug. She had never been sexed like this before—he seemed to be inexhaustible—she was reaching an eyrie of pleasure that nobody had ever taken her to before. Up, up, up, into a realm she'd only dreamed of.

And then there was her scream and his cry as they both died "the little death," as the French called orgasm. And for just a moment it was like a death, all else obliterated except for their head-spinning joy.

Fargo got back to his hotel room about midnight. He was tired and drunk. Between rounds of lovemaking, they'd imbibed more than a little rum.

He was just turning up the lamp when he realized that somebody had been in his room. His extra pair of boots was in the wrong corner and his Henry lay flat on the floor, not leaned against the wall.

He gave everything a superficial once-over, not in any

106

real shape to give the room the kind of detailed search it required. He was lucky to get his clothes and boots off before falling asleep.

Allie wasn't a patient woman.

Most people who knew her knew to get to the point of the story quickly or she'd start sighing, tapping her foot or even yawning in their faces.

No different when, as now, she was following somebody, in this case Nick Crowley.

The full moon was radiant; the coyotes sounded lonely, even gloomy; and her cute little nose was probably frozen permanently.

The only way she could restrain herself from galloping up behind him and shooting him was that if she shot him, she'd never find out where he'd hidden the money.

They were coming up to a long bend on this old road and she decided to fall back some. He was now moving at little more than a lope. She didn't want to accidentally run into him as soon as she reached the bend.

Slowing down made her all the more impatient.

Now she focused on the sheer, silver gleam of the pine trees and the pleasing smell of burning leaves somewhere in the distance.

Take your time, woman. The money's real close now. Real close.

She'd never killed anybody before. That gave her some pause. She tried to picture killing Nick, but couldn't imagine it. But if she was to take the money and not have him looking for her the rest of her life, what else could she do?

She was going into the bend now. And suddenly she noticed that one element of night noise was abruptly missing. The sharp sound of Nick's horse. No hooves smacking the hard ground.

As she came around the last part of the bend, she leaned forward and gaped. She couldn't believe what she saw. Or, more accurately, she couldn't believe what she didn't see. There was no sign of Nick at all.

She reined her horse in and sat there gaping around. Goose bumps covered her arms. But these weren't from the cold. These were from shock. Out here alone. Nobody around to help if she needed it. The woods on either side of the road looking more sinister than woods had ever looked to her.

And then a rustling came from behind her. And in the two seconds it took her to turn around, she pictured exactly what had happened.

She had a vivid image of Nick figuring out that she was behind him. And then an equally vivid image of Nick quickly hiding his horse in the woods before Allie came around the bend. And then—

His harsh, arrogant laugh. "Good thing you know what to do in bed, Allie. Otherwise I'd kill you right here."

And then she saw him emerging from the woods that came right up to the road on either side of her. He toted a carbine that was pointed right at her. "You planning on taking it all for yourself, Allie? You sure don't trust me much, do you?"

And then he brought his carbine up into firing position, sighted down the barrel and fired away.

33

The desk clerk was asleep. Sheriff Cordell didn't wake him up. He went behind the desk, took the extra key from the slot, and then walked over to the stairs.

The hotel, shoddily built, had as many late-night aches and pains as an old man. And then there was that chorus of various human bodies making various human noises. You worked in enough jails over your life, as Cordell had, and you got used to them.

When he found the room he wanted, he inserted the key he'd just taken and opened the door. He left the door open. He wanted spill light from the hall so he could see where he was going.

He saw the gleam of a gun barrel.

"You're not exactly delicate on your feet," Fargo said.

"I didn't get to finish ballerina school."

"Go over there and turn up the lamp."

"You're giving the orders now, huh, Fargo?" But he went over and turned up the lamp.

Fargo was sitting up in bed, Colt in hand. Cordell sat on the room's only chair.

Fargo put his gun on his lap and started rolling himself a smoke. "So why're you up here, Cordell?"

"Because I'm wondering if you killed Sievers."

Fargo whistled. "So they're turning on each other."

"Who're we talking about here?"

"Allie, Sievers and Crowley."

"What's their connection supposed to be?"

"That robbery downriver a few weeks ago."

"Where the soldiers were killed?"

"Yeah, and a lady friend of mine. Remember?"

The lawman scowled. "So what you're saying is that those three were the robbers?"

"Yeah. But I don't expect you to believe that."

"You saved me the time of saying that myself. Unless you've got some evidence, that is."

"Nothing that'd hold up in court as yet."

The lawman gave Fargo a long look. "You like Navajo jewelry?"

"You changing the subject?"

The sheriff shrugged. "A little bit."

"I have a good-fortune ring that a brave gave me for helping to find his little boy who got lost in a storm."

"You wear it?"

"No. I hate wearing jewelry. I keep it in my saddlebags."

"The bags over there?"

"Yeah. Why?"

Didn't take long for the sheriff to cross over to the far side of the bureau and hold up the saddlebags. "Don't worry. I won't steal anything."

"What the hell's this about?"

But the lawman finished his search before he said anything. Suddenly, the ring appeared between his fingers, popping up the way a magician would do it.

"This the ring you're talking about?"

"Yeah. Why?"

"The stone's missing."

The sheriff pitched the ring over to Fargo. Fargo looked it over.

"Somebody pried the stone from it." Then he remembered that somebody had been in his room earlier. "Somebody was in here tonight."

Sheriff Cordell reached into his coat pocket and took something out. He dropped the saddlebags back where they'd been. He came over to Fargo and handed him the stone he'd found near Sievers's body.

Fargo took one look at it in the palm of his hand and said, "Somebody wants to make you think I killed Sievers."

The sheriff went back to his chair and sat down. "That's one way of looking at it."

"Meaning I did it. You don't sound like you believe that."

"I don't, I guess. I can see where the stone was pried from the ring. Wouldn't make much sense for you to do something like that."

"It sure wouldn't."

"How's your memory?"

Fargo shook his head. "I'm sure Allie and Sievers and Nick Crowley were there that night. But I couldn't swear under oath that I remember anything. When I first saw them, only Allie looked a little bit familiar to me. And that didn't go anywhere. I didn't have any specific memories of her at all. Just this feeling that I'd seen her before."

"A federal man was through here yesterday. They need a witness. They haven't been able to dig up any other evidence about the robbers. You could make it easy for them."

"Yeah, if I could just remember."

"I guess it wouldn't do me any good to wire the federal man now. Not until you could help him for sure."

Two or three times a day his lost memory loomed on the edge of Fargo's consciousness. He sensed that everything he needed to know was just sitting there behind a closed door. If he could just figure out how to open that door . . .

Sheriff Cordell stood up. "I don't know about you, but I need my beauty sleep. I just wanted to clear my head and make sure you didn't have anything to do with killing Sievers." He walked to the door. "I'll have to think about those three. Maybe you're right. Maybe one of them killed Sievers to get another third of the money."

"Or maybe two of them killed Sievers."

"Maybe." The lawman gave a brief salute off the brim of his hat. "I'll talk to you some more in the morning."

"Very funny, you bastard."

Nick Crowley was still laughing.

"You could've killed me with those shots."

"Allie, if I'd wanted to kill you, you'd be dead by now. I heard you following me about an hour ago. That's why I veered right when we came to the stage road. I sure as hell wasn't going to take you to where I really hid the money."

"You mean this has been a wild-goose chase?"

"It sure has been." He laughed again.

They stood in the road next to their mounts. Their breaths came out in ghosts. The ripe smell of road apples was on the air thanks to the needs of Crowley's mount.

"I've got a right to know where that money is."

"So you could kill me and then run off with it?"

"How do I know you won't try the same thing on me?"

Nick Crowley took on the sound of a reasonable, wiser man than one would have expected to hear from a hooched-up troublemaker. He'd been using this tone on and off ever since the robbery. It was such bullshit it grated on Allie. Wisdom from Nick Crowley? Not likely.

"Allie, I'm doing this for our own safety. I'm not touching the money and you aren't either. And I don't have to tell you what'd happen if Sievers ever got his hands on it, do I?"

"You still haven't taken care of Fargo. And he's going

everywhere asking questions. He just might stumble onto something."

"He'll be dead by tomorrow night. I promise."

"He's a lot tougher than we thought he would be."

Crowley patted the carbine he'd stuffed back into its scabbard. "Not when I take half his head off with this rifle of mine."

"Just do it quick. He makes me nervous as hell."

Then, with no warning, she slapped him hard enough to snap his head back.

"What the hell was that for?" Crowley snarled.

"For this damned wild-goose chase tonight."

"I was just having a little fun with you." He gave her the leer he'd been polishing since he was ten years old and had semi-raped Natalie "Knickers" O'Toole in the old man's haymow.

"You can forget about that, Nick. You had your chance and you walked away from it."

"How about for old time's sake?"

"You're crazy. It took me a long time to get over you and I'm never going through that again."

He made his inevitable big, handsome guy move toward her.

She made a fist and drove it deep into his crotch.

He screamed louder than the coyotes.

He even did her the great favor of falling to his knees. "Damn you, Allie."

"I'm sick of telling you not to come sniffing around. I told you I got in on the robbery strictly for business reasons."

He still couldn't find the strength to stand up. He just held his crotch and moaned.

She turned her back on him, walked to her mount and climbed up on the big bay.

"You had that coming, Nick." Now it was her turn to laugh. "You better not stay out here all night, Nick. You might catch cold."

"You bitch!" he cried to her back as she rode away fast.

34

The first thing Fargo did in the morning was ride out to the Crowley spread. It was something out of a picture book. Vast grasslands, outbuildings that gleamed with new paint and a magnificent white three-story house that dominated everything else. There was a huge gazebo in back of the house, three cottages that would be for servants and guests alike, and a long shed that held four different types of carriages. There was an air of royalty about the place. Fargo wouldn't have been surprised to find men walking about in jodhpurs and riding to hounds. The men he did see were the two who let him in through the ornate black gates. One of them rode behind him with a sawed-off shotgun all the way to the house.

A Mexican woman answered Fargo's knock on the great, wide, matching front doors.

"I'd like to see Mr. Crowley, please."

"Do you have an appointment?"

"I'm afraid not. But I'm sure he'll see me."

She was a slender, elderly woman with a fierce, part-Indian face. Her dark eyes showed her contempt for mere mortals like Fargo. Many servants adopted their boss's arrogance as their own.

He was ultimately taken to a den where he had a few minutes to marvel at an enormous globe, photographs of two presidents signed to Crowley and a selection of Spanish daggers dating back three centuries.

Crowley came in wearing an expensive, custom-fitted white shirt and dark trousers. He seemed bigger, bolder than he had the first time Fargo met him. Maybe he did run the world, as the size of the globe suggested. He tried to break Fargo's hand when they shook. All he accomplished was bruising a couple of fingers.

They faced each other across a desk that was bigger than some ship decks Fargo had seen. Crowley offered a cigar, and smoked one himself when Fargo politely declined. The cigar, an expensive one of course, was diminished in size by Crowley's big hand.

"I'm glad you're here, Mr. Fargo. I was beginning to think you'd given up and were afraid to tell me about it."

Fargo shook his head. "If I was afraid to see you, it would have been because what I found out isn't something you'll want to hear."

Crowley scowled. "Shit." He stared through the mullioned window to his right. His scowl grew deeper. "He was involved in that robbery?"

"If I say yes, then it'll sound like I have solid proof. I don't. But from what I've been able to piece together, I'd have to say probably. He may even have killed Sievers."

"Sievers?" He not only scowled this time; he looked offended. "All my life I've tried to convince my boys that they only hang round respectable people. With Roger, there was never any problem. But with Nick—" He took a deep drag on his stogie. "Sievers was a lowlife."

"Your son knew him reasonably well."

"That part I knew. I talked to him and talked to him and he'd never listen. I'd always tell him that if he ever had any thought about becoming an honest citizen and giving up on his hooliganism, he'd have to get rid of all his friends. I'm not naive about my son, Mr. Fargo. I can't say that they dragged him down. In some cases, I'm sure he dragged them down. But still and all, a better group of friends might have helped him."

"How about Allie Blaine?"

Crowley snorted. "I'm surprised that a man like you doesn't recognize a chippie when he sees one. I'll grant you that she looks like a lost kitten, and you want to pick her up and pet her and help her in any way you can. But she's a cunning little tramp is all she is. People tell me that Nick broke her heart. I'm not sure she had any heart to break. As far as I'm concerned, she's no better than a whore. She's been with an awful lot of men. And when she met Nick she saw that she just might be able to settle him down a bit and get his money." A bitter smile. "But all Nick wanted from her was sex. And that's why she's so broken-hearted. She didn't get the fortune she'd set her sights on."

Fargo listened with increasing disappointment as Crowley kept finding reasons to exonerate his son. Seems it was the "bad influences" parents often used when they didn't want to face up to what kind of creature they'd raised. Sievers and Allie weren't exactly in the forefront of great human beings, but as for being a bad influence on Nick—pretty damned unlikely.

Fargo also realized that he'd brought the wrong news out here. The old man had hired him to find his son innocent. Any other report would be summarily rejected.

"That isn't his style," Crowley said. "Nick's, I mean. He's a hell-raiser. I won't deny that. And I admit I've had to pay a lot of money over the years to get him out of scrapes. But robbery—he's the son of the richest man in this part of the Territory. When I kick off, he and his brother Roger will have more money than anybody else out here. And they both know I've got more than my share of medical problems. All Nick has to do is straighten out his life and wait for my time to come. I cut him off but I'll be glad to write him back in as soon as he grows up a little."

Fargo started to speak but the old man stopped him.

"And what you brought me isn't evidence, Mr. Fargo. It's hearsay. And you pretty much admit that yourself—am I right?"

"We both agreed that it wouldn't stand up in court."

Crowley made a steeple of his two big hands and touched them to his chin, a contemplative pose for a man who didn't want to contemplate the truth. Not where his son was concerned, anyway.

"You know what, Mr. Fargo? I'm going to pay you off and throw in a small bonus. I'm not criticizing your work. You've done a hell of a lot better job than Cordell would have. But I'm beginning to see that it's a waste of time. I let gossip about Nick spook me. I started thinking that maybe he did have something to do with that robbery. And I think you let scuttlebutt do the same thing to you." He smiled. "He didn't have anything to do with that robbery, any more than you or I did."

He stood up with no warning. "Stay there. I've got a wall safe over here."

So that was that, Fargo thought. I wish I had enough to pay somebody to lie to me. Takes a rich man to do that.

Crowley swung a portrait of Washington back from the wall, revealing a large, circular safe. Crowley did a few turns to the right, a few turns to the left with the combination, and then swung the door open. He reached in and brought out two stacks of greenbacks that would probably keep Fargo in clean long johns for the rest of his life.

Crowley flipped through the edge of the stack, withdrew a number of bills and reversed the procedure with the safe. He brought the money over to Fargo. The bonus was more than Fargo had expected. But it was probably a small price for the pathetic peace of mind it would bring Crowley.

Fargo stood up. Crowley offered his hand as if they were businessmen concluding a business deal.

"Now make sure you have a good time spending that money, Mr. Fargo." A forced laugh. "And make sure that the bulk of it goes to the ladies. I never had the time for ladies. Did nothing but work my ass off most of those years. But now that I'm old, I sure look back and wish I'd spent a lot more time with the girls. I look at some of those young ones now and I damned near cry over what I've missed."

Fargo hadn't understood till now what a sad old bastard Crowley was. He felt sorry for him. You had to do a powerful lot of denying to think a bad apple like Nick Crowley was eventually going to turn into somebody worthwhile. That kind of denying takes a whole lot out of a man's soul.

Fargo was going to tell Crowley that he'd still be around town, still trying to fill in the blanks in his memory. But he was pretty sure that wasn't what Crowley wanted to hear. The more Fargo searched the more likely he would be to find out the truth about the robbery. And that meant the truth about Nick Crowley.

Fargo let himself out of the den and walked the well-polished hall to the front door, where the dour woman waited for him.

The tenderness in her voice was almost shocking. "I listened at the door, Mr. Fargo. No matter what you heard, he's a decent man. Nick has always made his life terrible. He keeps waiting for him to change. But he'll never change. And if it turns out that Nick is involved in that robbery"— she sounded on the verge of tears—"I really think Mr. Crowley would die. I think his heart would just give up."

Fargo put his hand on her shoulder and nodded. There was nothing to say.

He left.

Roger Crowley was just leaving one of those interminable meetings he enjoyed—he secretly judged staff members on how well they faked interest and enthusiasm during the dull forced-march lectures he subjected them to—when he saw Karl Haskins lurking near the office that Roger used most of the time. He looked as if he'd been crying. Two of the tellers were studying him, then glancing at each other and shaking their heads.

Karl came up to him and said, "I need to tell you something."

"Get hold of yourself," Roger whispered.

He led the way into the office, waited until Karl was inside, then closed the door quietly behind him. "What the hell is the matter with you?" Roger snapped. "You look like shit."

Karl said, "I told you Clemmons was on to something. He asked me about that profit and loss statement again. Maybe we should just come clean."

This was a test for Roger Crowley. He'd always been the past master of self-control, but he felt himself about to be overwhelmed by fear. And if he was overwhelmed, that would only send Karl into hysteria.

Roger started biting the inside of his cheek so angrily he drew blood. Beneath the surface of his desk, his fingers clawed the underside with such force that one of his nails snapped. He wanted to shout, to smash, to run out the door. But he couldn't. One of them had to remain calm. Had to. No choice in the matter.

"You're supposed to be the one with all the answers, Roger, tell me what to do."

And then it came out. An answer. The answer. There waiting all the time. "I know exactly what we do."

"Then tell me, Roger, tell me."

Roger was afraid Karl really was going to weep. God, why did he ever agree to such a stupid plan with such a stupid man?

"We kidnap Nick."

"Nick?" Karl looked stunned. "He'd kill us."

"You make him sound invincible. He isn't. He usually eats at the café and then goes back to his sleeping room for a nap. And then he goes out for a night of raising hell. That gives us plenty of possibilities to find him."

"So we kidnap him and then what?"

"Then we give him a choice. Either he tells us where the money is or we kill him."

"You'd kill your own brother?"

Roger smiled. "You ever remember him *treating* me like a brother?"

A modicum of composure had returned to Karl's face. "I guess we don't have any choice."

"We sure as hell don't."

"I'm sorry I got so crazy."

"We have a plan now. You can relax. By tomorrow morning, you can return the money to the accounts you took it from. He won't have time to go through everything today."

"He's got an important meeting at three this afternoon, anyway."

"See, right there. He's just shooting his mouth off. You can relax now."

"I still can't see Nick telling us anything. And if we kill him, he couldn't tell us even if he wanted to."

Roger smiled again. "I guess you've got a good point there. If he's dead, he can't talk."

Karl blushed. He hated Roger making fun of him. "You know what I mean, Roger."

"You're making him invincible again. We capture him, we tie him up and we torture him. He'll talk. He won't have any choice."

"He's tough."

"Not that tough. Nobody is. I remember reading an article in *Harper's* one time about how soldiers on both sides of the war—North and South alike—broke down after they'd been knocked around for a while. And not that long, either. We're not built for punishment, Karl. Maybe he can take it longer than we could but that still doesn't mean he can take it for very long."

"I just hope you're right. I've never been this scared in my life. I almost pissed my pants when I was leaving the office."

Roger laughed. "You didn't really need to tell me that, now, did you, Karl?"

For the first time during the visit, Karl smiled. "No, I probably should have kept that to myself, I guess."

Roger stood up. "I've got a lot of work ahead of me this afternoon. I need to dig in. You go back to work and stay calm. You can't afford to make Mr. Clemmons any more suspicious than he might be now."

"I know you're right about that. But it'll be tough."

Just before he opened the door for his old friend, Roger said, "And whatever you do, Karl, don't piss your pants. On that gray suit of yours, it'll be pretty obvious you had an accident."

Karl looked embarrassed. "I really shouldn't have told you that, should I?"

35

When he came in sight of Allie Blaine's small house, Fargo reined in his Ovaro stallion. He knew instantly that something was wrong. A ground-tied horse stood to the right of the house, and the front door was open. The temperature was hovering just above forty. Why would the door be open when it was this chilly?

He didn't have time for any more thinking. A quick carbine shot from within the shadows of the doorframe knocked off his hat, and a second shot grazed his left temple. Ordinarily he would have jumped from his horse, but the grazing bullet packed enough power to knock him to the ground, slamming the back of his head hard against the dead yellow grass.

He got up to his knees and slapped his stallion across the flanks to drive it away so it wouldn't get wounded or killed. Then he rolled to a group of tree stumps. Lots of such stumps around here, the remains of the Dakota frontier being settled for farmhouses and farm families.

A stump gave him enough protection, when he lay flat, to send three bullets from his Colt into the shadowy doorframe of the house.

But even as he fired, Fargo was aware that something strange had happened.

He was Fargo, meaning that his memory had returned full-bore. He wasn't just the name Fargo; he was a man with a history, that history including the robbery of the army money and the murder of Amy. The rest of that missing forty-eight hours fell into place as well. Making love to Amy. Preparation on the boat. The shoot-out.

It was all there, unbidden, as if some celestial force had simply flipped a switch of some kind.

He'd assumed, ever since he'd been knocked off his stallion, that the shooter was Allie. But then he glimpsed the ground-tied horse again. Not Allie's horse. And, he reasoned, probably not Allie firing at him.

Now he wondered who the hell was in that house.

He was momentarily pulled between the deep pleasure of getting his memory back and taking care of the shooter. But pleasing as his fleshed-out memory was, the shooter came first.

He remembered the creek to the west of the house. Shallow creek but steep banks. His only hope of getting the shooter. He squeezed off two shots and began rolling the ten yards to the top of the creek bank.

The shooter was well aware of what Fargo was trying to do. He pumped five bullets in the direction of Fargo's rolling body. Fargo knew his only chance was to keep rolling. He didn't so much as pause when he reached the edge of the bank. He just allowed himself to drop the five feet down into the narrow creek below. The water was cold as hell, and just as he was climbing out of it, the slight wound where the bullet had grazed him started to sting.

He was pretty much soaked as he ran splashing through two feet of clear water. He had an idea. Whether it would work or not, it was the only idea he could come up with. It had damned well better work.

When he reached a point that brought him to the back of the house, he started checking his bullets. He'd held his Colt out of the water when he rolled off the bank, so the gun was no problem.

He stood up once to check out what was going on behind Allie's house. A small screen door opened onto a small garden and an outhouse.

Would the shooter respond as Fargo hoped he would? And would Fargo have enough bullets to fool the shooter and then kill him if need be?

At this point, Fargo knew he had no choice but to see if his plan worked.

He crouched down on the angled red clay bank. His hat was off. His lake blue eyes fixed on the back door of the place. And then he fired a couple of shots. Even from here, he could hear them rip through the wood of the rear door.

Now he had to hurry, put the second part of his plan to work.

Karl Haskins, the son-in-law of the second-richest man in the Territory, put his head down on his desk and began to sob. His father-in-law, B. F. Clemmons, had often accused him of marrying his daughter Ellen for her money. Clemmons, who was also Karl's employer, was about to get the evidence he needed to prove that.

The worst part of it was that he could hear two of the secretaries just outside his door, whispering about whether they should knock or not.

There was no way he could let them in. His eyes would be red, his nose running and his voice would sound like a woman's—exactly the way his wife carried on after he'd beaten her for fifteen minutes or so.

But he couldn't stop crying. The harder he tried to stop, the more he blubbered.

And then—the very worst thing of all—he'd have to walk out there and let them all look at him. The boss. The man who liked to crack down just to show he had authority. The man who brooked no excuses for being late, sick or having any kind of family troubles.

Sobbing. In his office.

And then he remembered the location of that office.

He turned in his leather executive swivel chair and looked at the wooden louvers that covered his rear window, said window opening on the lot where he parked his buggy every day.

He started snuffling up his tears. There was a way out of here after all—and nobody could see him. Out the rear window and into his buggy and out of here, leaving a note on his desk that he was afraid he had come down with the influenza that had been so troublesome since the weather

122

had changed. He would say that he liked all of them so much that he just didn't want to see any of them get sick.

Would they think he was noble?

For an instant—one of those giddy moments when the mind cranks out ridiculous ideas that sound tremendously, reasonably effective for about 1.3 seconds—he thought they'd probably stand around and say he wasn't such an SOB after all. He cared so much about our health that he climbed out the back window.

What a tremendous human being he is.

Then the 1.3 seconds were up.

There was no note that could possibly explain his behavior to these gossipy, incompetent assholes.

He'd just have to come back tomorrow and tell them that he'd stopped at the telegrapher's on his way to work and picked up a telegram that informed him of the death of a cousin who'd always been like a sister to him. And if they didn't like it, to hell with them.

He'd have the money replaced in the accounts and he'd be back in the good graces of Clemmons and to hell with them.

He then proceeded to remind himself that he had never been very good at any endeavor that required grace or skill. Or climbing. He'd always burned his thighs on rope climbing, and fallen out of any tree he'd magically managed to climb.

As soon as he moved the wooden louvers back and started to slide the window up, he felt the tightness of his suit. He took off his jacket and vest. Still pretty tight. His clothes inhibited his struggle through the window frame. But what the hell was he going to do—climb out the window naked?

He dragged a straight-backed chair over after shoving the window up. He'd have to be quick. Clemmons always took his lunch at eleven instead of noon. He frequently used the alley here to return.

He went to work—clumsy, sweaty, dirty-word-saying, pants-tearing work. At one point he was vised in so tight in the frame that he wondered if he'd ever be able to escape. Lord, wouldn't that be embarrassing, having to get the janitor or the handyman to come and set him free? There would be whispers and snickers for months, maybe years.

And then he got free.

He got so free, in fact, that before he could situate himself comfortably in the open window, he fell straight down to the ground and cried out when he felt one of his ribs crack.

But that wasn't the worst of it. Oh, no. He'd been so attentive to his escape that he hadn't paid any attention to the alley.

He hadn't noticed that Mr. B. F. Clemmons had, in fact, been watching this ridiculous employee of his perform this ridiculous trick of somehow laboring his way through the window but then falling out of it.

"I think even my daughter will give up protecting you this time, Karl," the stout man said, and then stalked down the alley to the street side so he could enter his bank through the front door.

36

Fargo could hear the shooter inside stumbling into furniture as he made his way to the back door, where it would be his obvious intention to take on Fargo.

The problem with that intention was that Skye wouldn't be there to be fired upon.

As soon as he'd tricked the shooter into firing out the back door, Fargo hunched over and made a run down the creek bank. Then he scrambled up the bank, hurled himself onto the grass and broke into a run directly toward the small house.

Enough time had passed that the shooter had to be having second thoughts about firing out the back door. There had been no response from Fargo. What did that mean? Had he wounded Fargo, maybe even killed him? Was Fargo simply waiting him out before he started firing again?

Or had he—

But even if the shooter had been smart enough to realize that he'd been duped, he was too late as Fargo rushed in the front door and said, "Drop the rifle or you're dead."

He'd already been able to see that the shooter was none other than the infamous Nick Crowley.

But almost as soon as he figured out who the man was, his attention strayed to the dead woman propped up in the corner. Nick Crowley hadn't taken any chances. He'd shot her in the forehead and the right eye.

Crowley turned around, holding the carbine high.

"Set it down easy on the table there." Fargo nodded to Allie. "You don't mind shooting women, huh, Crowley?"

"Bullshit," Crowley said. "That's why I was shootin' at you. I figured you were the killer."

"Sure you did."

"I didn't have any reason to kill her."

"Of course not. Probably never entered your mind that if you killed Sievers and Allie you'd have all the money to yourself."

"I didn't kill Sievers, either."

"You still haven't put the carbine down."

"Oh." Crowley sounded and looked genuinely surprised. "I forgot." He set it down without any problem.

Fargo had never spoken to Crowley before, but he'd formed an opinion of the big young man as being not only arrogant but trigger-prone, too. This Crowley was very different from that one. Fargo had a thought that shocked him. Could Crowley here be telling the truth? Hadn't he killed either Allie or Sievers?

"Tell me what happened when you rode up."

"Nothing happened, Fargo. I rode up and knocked on the door. It swung open. It hadn't been closed all the way.

I called her name and then I came inside. She was just the way you see her now."

"You didn't see anybody else around?"

"No. But then you came up. I figured you saw me here and came back to kill me, too."

"You thought I killed her?"

"Hell, yes. Everybody knows why you're here. You're trying to remember what happened."

"I've got news for you, Crowley. I do remember what happened. And I remember seeing you, Sievers and Allie there that night of the robbery. Sievers did most of the shooting."

"You sure as hell can't prove it."

"I don't need to prove it," Fargo said. Time to pull another trick on Crowley. "I'm just going to kill you the way I killed Sievers and Allie."

"See, I knew you killed them."

Fargo raised his Colt and leveled it directly at Crowley's chest.

Crowley said, "I didn't kill any of them that night."

"You're lying."

"Listen to me, dammit." He was losing his nerve, his style. "You think I'm stupid enough to kill soldiers and have the *federales* after me? I told Sievers over and over not to kill anybody."

Fargo smiled. "You just admitted to the robbery and murder."

"Murder, my ass, Fargo. I told you it was Sievers."

"Maybe so, Crowley. But you need to read a law book sometime. You're up for three murder charges, too."

"You're forgetting something, Fargo."

"Yeah? Like what?"

"Like my old man. You think he'd let me hang? He probably wouldn't even let me go to prison."

"Your old man can't control the court system."

Crowley laughed. He sounded like every gunnie punk-ass braggart Fargo had ever run into.

"You don't know my old man."

Fargo squeezed off two quick shots. One of them came so close to Crowley's ear that it must have singed it. Crowley dropped to the floor. He screamed like a ten-year-old.

Gun smoke and bullet echo filled the area. Crowley whimpered like a kicked dog.

"Even if they don't hang you, Crowley, a pretty boy like you'll have a whole lot of fun in prison."

"You son of a bitch."

Memories of Amy were vivid with Fargo now. That face. That laugh. That sudden and surprising tenderness. "Get up before I kill you."

"You son of a bitch."

Fargo was sick of him. He took three steps and jammed the edge of his boot smack into Crowley's sullen mouth. But that wasn't enough, not with Amy's memory so pure and fine and melancholy on his mind. The next thing that cracked was Crowley's nose. Blood shot straight out of both nostrils. His hands covered his face. Redness ran down his fingers.

The sobbing was louder than the gunshots or the bones snapping.

Fargo kicked Crowley his gun. "Pick it up, gunnie. Let me make it legal."

Crowley took his hands from his face. Blood hung in thick blotches from both his nose and mouth. He was a mess. His eyes burned with rage and fear. He looked down at his trembling right hand as if it wasn't attached to his body but was something just floating past him. It was easy to see he was calculating a way to pick up his gun and kill Fargo before Fargo killed him.

Fargo wasn't done yet. He held his Colt up as if showing it off to a prospective buyer, side to side, as if declaiming on its beauty and utility. Then he set it carefully down on the table.

"You've got a pretty good chance of killing me, Crowley. And it's your last chance."

Crowley, all bloody, shaking, muttering curses, began the laborious work of picking up a body that was not as dependable as usual. The pain from his mouth and nose was damned near blinding. He felt the humiliating need to talk to his dead mother. How had his world, a world he'd ruled since he was a boy, ever come to this? Nobody had ever spoken to him the way Fargo had. Nobody had ever beaten and injured him the way Fargo just had.

And there was the gun that could win it all back for him. Pride. Revenge. Freedom.

The gun. His gun. No more than three inches from his hand.

Could he pick it up before Fargo got his own weapon and emptied its contents into Crowley? Because he had no doubt that was what Fargo wanted to do. Put not just one or two slugs into him, but empty the whole mother lode into his body.

He raised his eyes to meet Fargo's and then had the disturbing notion that maybe he wasn't looking at a sane man. Maybe the loss of the woman at the boat had completely undone him. Maybe he was looking at a man who didn't give a damn if he died as long as he got to see Crowley die first.

No doubt Fargo was fast. But he did have to reach across for the gun. That would add two seconds at the very least to fitting gun to hand. And then a second to turn, aim and fire. Maybe two seconds. Would that give Crowley the advantage he needed?

But then all of Crowley's calculations became moot because in the doorway behind Fargo stepped what at first seemed to be an apparition. He wanted to wipe the sweat from his eyes to make sure that what he was seeing was real.

No. Impossible.

"Much as I'd like you to kill him, Mr. Fargo, I'm afraid I'll have to deprive you of that privilege. At least for now." Then, looking over his shoulder, "Get in here, Karl, and tie both of them up."

Roger Crowley came inside the house quickly.

Even before Fargo had time to turn around completely, Roger angled his carbine around and cracked Fargo across the back of the head with it.

Fargo was unconscious before he hit the floor.

37

Karl Haskins was self-conscious about tying people up. He'd been raised to be polite. He'd been raised not to inflict injury or discomfort on people. He'd been raised to say please and thank you.

So it wasn't surprising that as he cinched the rope around Nick Crowley's wrists and ankles, he said, "This'll probably hurt you a little, I guess." He didn't want to apologize because that would make him feel foolish. Either you tied up a man or you didn't. But maybe by mumbling these words both he and Nick would feel better about it.

"It's going to be a pleasure to kill you, Karl. A real pleasure."

"I'm just doing what your brother told me to."

"My brother." Nick spat the word out. "You're afraid of my brother?"

"We're in this thing together, me and Roger, I mean."

"What thing?"

Roger, who was tying up the unconscious Skye Fargo, said, "Will you shut the hell up, Haskins? Our business isn't any of his."

"Sorry," Karl said.

He chastised himself even as he spoke. Where was the fire that was always there when he was beating up his wife and raining down on his employees? Maybe it was because of the way he'd been crying in his office with the secretaries listening, or maybe it was falling out of the window with

Clemmons looking on. Or maybe it was because Fargo, even unconscious, looked like one of the meanest bastards he'd ever seen. And that wasn't to overlook Nick here. He'd been afraid of Nick ever since they were boys.

"How come you killed Allie?" Karl asked.

Nick said, "I didn't kill Allie, you moron. And you better tell me what you and my brother are up to."

"You should see your face," Roger snapped. "You wouldn't be threatening anybody if I held a mirror up to you. Fargo here sure put you through it."

"Yeah, and he's going to pay for it, believe me." Nick didn't seem to realize that he sounded as if he had a cleft palate. His front teeth were busted and sticking out. His lip was badly cut. He had blood in his throat. He sounded like some kind of circus freak.

Roger laughed. "I wouldn't talk if I was you, Nick. You sound stupid."

But Nick's temper wouldn't let him shut up. He was so used to trying to intimidate people that even when he sounded humorously injured he couldn't shut up. "I'm not kidding here, Roger."

"We'll see," Roger said, finished now with tying up Fargo.

"My ass we'll see. The only way out of this for you is to tell Karl here to untie me, and then you two head back to town and we'll forget this whole thing."

Karl glanced at Roger. He'd never seen Roger look so stern. This was a different Roger. Roger had the fire now and it pissed Karl off. Why didn't Karl have the fire? Why couldn't he pretend he was beating up his wife when he was cinching up Nick? Hell, at the moment, Nick couldn't do a damn thing about it.

"Don't pay any attention to him, Karl. You just go see how that thing is outside."

Karl almost swore. He knew that Roger would go back on his word. Roger had promised him that he wouldn't have to handle it at all.

"Why don't you go look at it yourself?"

"That's it, Karl," Nick said through his bloody mouth. "Stick up for yourself."

And then Nick cried out. The pain left. The pain returned. Ebb and flow.

"My nose!" he shouted. And he started kicking his feet, with their bound ankles, against the floor in a tantrum.

"You're my brother. You gotta help me with my nose."

Roger said, "I'm talking to Karl here. So you just shut up."

Nick started crying. The pain was on him bad now, really bad. The blood in his throat sounded terrible, a ghoulish gurgling sound. People choked on blood in their throats this way.

Roger said calmly, "I'll go see how things are. You just hold your gun on him."

Karl nodded. "I tied him up pretty tight."

"Don't take any chances. If he starts to work those ropes off, kick him in the nose. That'll keep him quiet."

Karl smiled nervously. "So much for brotherly love, I guess."

Roger said, "That went out the window a long time ago."

After Roger left, Nick asked, "What's he got outside?"

"Just be quiet."

Fargo groaned. In order to see him, Karl had to angle himself away from Nick, which made him uncomfortable. If anybody could escape being tied that tight, it was Nick. He walked over to Fargo quickly.

Fargo said, "You hold that gun like you're scared of it."

"I can shoot you full of lead if that's what you're worried about."

"And you'd better keep a close eye on Nick over there."

"You don't worry about Nick, either."

"Kill him now, Karl," Nick said. "He's trouble for all of us. Maybe me and Roger can work out some kind of deal. Fargo'd just be in the way. He wants all of us dead."

"Don't listen to him, Karl," Fargo said. His head pounded. Every time he moved, the rough hemp of his bondage tore off a layer of skin. "The only one I want to kill is Nick. You and Roger I don't care about."

"That's a crock," Nick said.

The way Karl kept whipping his head back and forth to look at each man was almost funny. He looked like a little

131

kid trapped between two huge, angry adults. He wasn't sure which to believe, which to be more frightened of. He didn't even notice that the gun in his hand had begun to droop lower. He was one inattentive gunman, that was for sure.

A yelp came from outside.

"What was that?" Nick asked.

"I better go see," Karl said.

"Roger'll probably want you to stay in here," Fargo said.

"Go see what's wrong with him," Nick said.

"I sure wouldn't leave my post, Karl," Fargo said. "He might have a knife and cut the ropes."

"He's just worried I'll kill him if I get set free," Nick said. "Now go see what happened to my brother, dammit."

"Stay here, Karl. Don't take the chance on letting him go."

Karl couldn't take it anymore. He clamped his hands over his ears and said, "Shut up!"

Roger came back in. He seemed fine. He shook his head when he saw Karl with his hands over his ears. Then Karl saw him and quickly put his hands down.

"What the hell's going on in here?"

"They're driving me crazy is what's going on. Nick wanted me to go outside and see if you were okay. And Fargo told me to not leave my post."

Roger laughed. "C'mon, Karl, even you can figure that one out. They're each trying to use you. Whichever one of them got free first, the other one is dead."

There was such certainty, such swagger in the new Roger that Karl found himself not liking his longtime friend at all. He sounded more and more like his brother, Nick. And acted that way, too. Now, when he spoke to Karl, he spoke in the same arrogant way Nick always had to both of them. Karl felt confused and lonely, and wondered for the first time if it all wouldn't be better if he simply rode back to town and told Clemmons the truth—and faced whatever consequences came along. He had a glimpse into the future.

With Roger acting this way, and two men like Fargo and Nick involved, there was no way this situation could turn out well. No way at all.

38

Sheriff Cordell was working on paperwork when his deputy knocked on his door and said that B. F. Clemmons wanted to see him.

"What the hell does he want?" Cordell asked from behind his desk.

"Wouldn't tell me. Said it was none of my business."

"That sounds like him, all right. Well, bring him back."

There were six men on the town council. When the senior Crowley had served on it, his was the most powerful and singular voice. But since his son Nick had gotten in so much trouble, Crowley got too embarrassed to show up and make excuses—or pay his fines. He claimed he had too much else to do, what with his various businesses and all, so he dropped out of council meetings. Clemmons, the second-wealthiest man in town, had gladly taken Crowley's place. The irritating thing was that the senior Crowley had rarely forced decisions on the council. There were some things, of course, that he had simply demanded be done, and they had been done. But mostly Crowley had let the council function democratically, or at least as democratically as such councils ever function. There were distinct good sides and bad sides to Crowley, and the council members had mostly seen the good sides.

With Clemmons there was a bad side and a worse side.

Clemmons came with his own agenda, passed copies of it around, then sat down and proceeded to work his own wants and needs. The other members tried to work theirs in but they rarely had time to speak because Clemmons— whom most of them owed loan money—generally picked up and left once he got his own business done.

Now he stood in Cordell's doorway, a walrus of a man, and said, "The last time I was here I walked in on you with your feet on the desk and a cigar in your mouth. Glad to see you've learned your lesson."

The last time you were in here, Cordell thought, you had a cob up your ass, and if I'm not mistaken, you've now got two cobs up your ass.

But Clemmons ruled the council and the council paid Cordell's salary, so all Cordell said was, "How can I help you today, B. F.?" Knowing full well that B. F. was not at all how "Mr. Clemmons" preferred to be addressed.

"I want you to find and arrest Karl Haskins."

"Our Karl Haskins? The fella who flinches if you even lean too close to him? When did he become a dangerous criminal?"

"I didn't ask for humor. I want him arrested."

"And that would be for what exactly?"

"For"—he paused—"for strange and very suspicious behavior."

"I see."

"I don't appreciate smirkers."

"I didn't realize I was smirking."

"Well, you were and I don't like it one damned bit."

Cordell sighed. "How about some background on this?"

He got his background. He also got a huge temptation that he had to struggle with to banish. The image of Karl Haskins falling out a window at the back of the bank almost inspired one hell of a long, hearty laugh. But he knew better. Clemmons might not fire him but he would most definitely send one of his notorious memos to the council, advising members that if Sheriff Cordell ever again acted in a less than courteous way to Clemmons, he would find his ass six counties away.

"How can I arrest him?"

"You're the sheriff, aren't you?"

"Yeah, but I didn't write the penal code. What's he done besides falling out a window?"

"Acted very suspiciously that's what he's done."

"I'm sorry, Mr. Clemmons," he said respectfully, "but that isn't enough. Now if you found something wrong with the books—"

"That's what we'll call it then. Suspicion of embezzlement." It was now Clemmons's turn to smirk. "Is that suitable enough for you, Mr. Sheriff?"

"That's enough."

"I'm glad it meets your high standards."

No, Cordell thought, I was mistaken. It's not two cobs you have up your ass. It's three.

"Now you start looking for him right away."

"Of course I will."

"And I want a report three hours from now, even if you haven't found him. I want a list of all the places you've looked."

Would you like that in Latin or Greek, you stinking bastard?

"Seems reasonable to me, Mr. Clemmons."

"It's very reasonable, Cordell. Especially if you want to hang on to your job in this town."

And with that, he was gone, off to spread sunshine elsewhere.

When the Crowley boys were still in grade school, Nick Crowley inadvertently revealed one area of vulnerability to his brother. They were rolling down a grassy hill, trying to see who could reach the bottom first, when Nick suddenly started screaming. He leaped to his feet and then started doing a frenzied dance, his face ugly with fear.

Roger would always remember the moment because it told him that there was one way he could completely incapacitate his brother. Put a snake in front of him.

The snake that sunny July afternoon had been a garter snake. But it might as well have been one of those exotic and deadly boa constrictors the adventure magazines were always writing about.

It was merely a garter snake.

Three times in the ensuing years, at times when he was exceedingly pissed off at Nick, Roger had planted snakes in his boots, his bed and his bureau drawer. Harmless snakes, the ugliest of which—it spooked even Roger, who had no particular fear of snakes—was a filthy, verminous-looking milk snake.

There was one trouble with this form of vengeance. Once the snake was disposed of, once Nick had had time to calm down, there was bloody hell to pay in the form of beatings such as only Nick could deliver.

Today, being dragged from Allie's house, Nick listened as Roger described in detail the prairie rattlesnake he'd caught and put in a deep hole he'd dug just outside the house.

Poor Nick went insane. Roger and Karl had a hard time keeping hold of him the way he was thrashing around, all the while sobbing and screaming and cursing. His face glistened with sweat. Spittle bubbled out of both sides of his mouth. His eyes had turned a rheumy red.

The snake, a heavily armored creature whose dark brown flesh allowed it to hide easily in most places on the prairie, cooperated by starting to hiss and rattle even before they'd reached it. Roger had secured the snake in the three-foot hole by sliding a sheet of wood across the opening and then setting three bricks on top of the wood. The snake was going nowhere, not until Roger wanted it to.

Fargo heard Nick's cries. He wasn't surprised by them. Every human being had at least one fear that turned him into a gibbering coward. Fargo had one, too, of course. A popular one, as it turned out. There had been so many examples of people being buried alive that the entire country had become fixated on the subject. Including Fargo. He had frequent nightmares of waking up inside a coffin, trying desperately to claw his way to freedom, but ultimately, his voice so hoarse that he could no longer even scream, just giving in to the suffocation that would soon claim his life.

So even though he hated Nick Crowley, Fargo knew the terror Nick was living right now, with Roger—as Roger had lovingly explained to Nick a few minutes before dragging him outside—about to slide back the wood covering the hole just far enough so that he could push his brother's face into the opening.

It wouldn't be long now. Fargo could tell that they were getting near the snake. The screaming had gotten even louder. These thoughts were on Fargo's mind as he whirled the rowels of his spurs against the ropes on his wrists. He had swung his legs up from the knees, moved his hands close to the rowels and started sawing away.

The process wasn't a quick one. All he could do was hope that they stayed busy for a while with Nick and his snake.

39

"He should be back any minute now, Sheriff," Clem at the livery told Cordell. "Just down the street havin' coffee."

"Fine, Clem. You go on about your work. I'll just sit here and wait."

Clem, who doubled as a vet when local farmers didn't want to pay a vet's prices, had just gotten back to town and had no idea if Karl Haskins, who boarded his horse there, had stopped by that morning or not. Frank Edwards, the morning man who was now on his break, would be back in a few minutes. He'd know for sure.

The lawman's thoughts were on the robbery and triple murder again. For one of the few times in his life, he found himself feeling sorry for Old Man Crowley. He was a regular gent compared to the new breed of rich man, Clemmons. Clemmons had come from money. He was like a man raised as a prince, so rising to the throne of his kingdom was no great honor. But Crowley had come from nothing. He appreciated the lives of common folks.

And he was about to get his heart broken.

Even without a memory, this Fargo was a smart, cunning and formidable man. He was going to find out who'd robbed the boat that night. Who'd killed those three people. And Cordell had no doubt that one of the criminals would turn out to be Nick, who had finally done what his longtime observers had always predicted he would do—maybe what Old Man Crowley himself had predicted he would do—and that was to get all bound up in a crime so heinous that no amount of Crowley money or influence could help him. Heartbreak was bad enough when you were young. But when you were old, like Crowley Senior . . .

The subject was so heavy on Cordell's mind that he went back to amusing himself with images of Karl Haskins falling out a window at the rear of the bank. It was also funny to imagine Clemmons's face while he watched this. The nasty bastard was lucky he hadn't died of a heart attack on the spot. His face turned bloodred whenever he got unduly angry. It stayed that way for several dangerous minutes, even after he'd calmed down. And the picture of poor ineffectual Karl tumbling out a window—Cordell laughed out loud. Just couldn't help it.

But something was going on. He'd been a lawman too long, in too many towns, not to hear the silent but real call of trouble. Karl Haskins acting the way he had this morning was damned near unthinkable. If he couldn't find Karl pretty soon, he'd see if Roger Crowley knew what was going on. Those two were more like brothers than Roger and Nick had ever been. If anybody knew what was wrong with Karl it would be Roger. But would Roger break confidence? Outsiders tended to stick together and those two sure were outsiders in every sense of the word. Not even their money and power had made them acceptable to the town elite. They would always be subjects of the quiet snicker and the whispered insult.

He'd just gotten his pipe going when he saw Frank Edwards waving to him. Cordell had parked his butt on a bale of hay out front of the livery so he could enjoy the parade of wagons and horses and people on the street. Great place for gaping.

"Howdy, Frank."

"Sure don't know how you get that pipe of yours to smell so good. Mine smells like I'm smoking rat turds."

"Gosh, I'll have to get me one like that."

"Always a kidder, ain't you?"

Cordell stood up. "Did Karl Haskins come in here this morning?"

"Yep. Just about noon." Frank, a man with an Adam's apple the size of a small, real apple, shook his head. "Seemed real strange. Then Roger Crowley saw him saddling up and swung over."

"You hear anything they said?"

Frank shrugged. "Somethin' about Allie, I guess. Heard Roger mention Nick, too, come to think of it."

"Allie, huh?"

Frank made a face. "She sure didn't turn out the way anybody around here hoped. She was such a sweet little thing when she was growin' up. And so pretty, too. Still pretty, I guess, but once she fell in with Nick . . . Say, by the way, any news on Sievers yet?"

"He's still dead."

Frank laughed. "There you go again."

Cordell tucked his pipe in the pocket of his suit coat and said, "Better be pushin' on, Frank. See you later."

"Hey, do me a favor, Sheriff."

"Sure."

"Don't ever tell anybody what I said about Allie. She had a pretty scrappy childhood and all. Maybe I'da turned out the same way if I'd been through what she has."

Cordell smiled at Frank and said, "You're a good fella, Frank. You know that?"

Frank grinned. "Sure wish you'd tell my wife that sometime."

"Are you ready?" Roger Crowley snapped. His aggravated tone was a response to Karl Haskins's nervous demeanor now that they had reached the pit with the snake in it. Roger had a second problem. He knelt next to the wooden cover, ready to push his brother's face into the hole once Haskins pulled the cover back. But brother wasn't cooperating. Brother was performing some spectacular gymnastics was what brother was doing. Even lying on the ground, even trussed up wrist and ankle, brother was managing to squirm, wriggle, wiggle, twist, thrash and otherwise make Roger's work difficult if not impossible. "Are you ready, Karl?" he screamed at Haskins.

"You really want to do this, Roger?" Karl asked, staring down at the squirming Nick. "Maybe the snake'll really bite him or something."

Maybe the snake'll really bite him or something.

Roger had been idly thinking about killing Karl once they found out where Nick had stashed the money, but his thoughts were idle no longer. No way could he travel with Karl. Now that they were up against it—now that they had the opportunity to be free of the community that had always scorned them, now that they had their chance to flee their dreary family lives—Karl was caving in, imploding.

Roger grabbed Nick's hair hard and shoved him closer to the pit. Below, the snake began rattling and hissing again. It was one angry sumbitch.

"Pull that cover back, Karl, and do it now!"

"No!" Nick cried. "No! You're my brother, Roger! You can't do this!"

"Oh, sure, I almost forgot. We're brothers, aren't we? And you've always treated me so well. Haven't you, brother dear?" He raised his head from his wriggling brother to Karl. "Do it now, Karl. You hear me? Now!" Then, staring down at his brother's sweaty, aggrieved face: "Tell me where the money is, Nick. Or I stick your head into that pit."

"I got that money. It's mine. I'll split it with you but you can't have it all."

Roger laughed. "You seem to think you're in some kind of bargaining position, brother dear. But you're not. Maybe I'll cut you in and maybe I won't. But right now the only way you can save yourself is to tell me where you put the money."

Just as Roger glanced up to speak to Karl, he saw the flash of metal in the sunlight—a six-shooter in Karl's hand.

"I don't want to put him down there, Roger."

"You forgetting the way he treated us all our lives?"

"No, I'm not forgetting that. But I don't have the stomach for seeing you put his face in that hole."

Roger smirked. "You have the stomach for beating up your wife, though, don't you, Karl?"

"That's none of your business."

"Help me, Karl," Nick said. "There's plenty of money. Convince Roger of that. There's plenty of money."

"You'd better tell me where it is, then, Nick," Roger said. "And, Karl, put that gun away. You look stupid standing there like that. You're not going to shoot anybody."

"I don't want you to put his head in that hole," Karl said.

"Then I'll move the damned cover myself."

"Shoot him, Karl. This is your last chance."

Roger leaned forward, his hand about ready to touch the edge of the cover and push it away.

"No!" Nick screamed. A kind of madness gave his eyes an unreal gleam now. His mind raced with images of a mythic serpent big enough to crush a man in its coils . . . waiting for him in that pit. "No!"

"Then where's the money!" Roger shouted at him, nudging the cover a half inch over the hole.

"Shoot him, Karl! Shoot him, you stupid, ugly bastard!"

And there it was. The entire history of these three men. "You stupid, ugly bastard." The same phrase they'd heard over and over.

Roger was startled by it at first but he quickly saw the effect the words had had on Karl. Roger started smiling. "You want to pull the cover back for me now, Karl?"

"I didn't mean anything by that," Nick said. The desperation in his tone said it all. "It just slipped out. I didn't mean to say it, Karl. I swear I didn't."

"Push his head in there good and deep," Karl said angrily.

He was just putting a toe to the cover to push it partially away from the hole when he raised his head and cried, "No!" The six-shooter he'd been holding went flying from his hand. A bullet had taken a piece of his thumb. He grabbed the thumb as if he'd been mortally wounded.

"Stand up easy," Fargo said from behind Roger, "and drop your gun."

Roger started to turn, apparently thinking of firing on Fargo, but Fargo said, "Don't be stupid. I'll kill you where you stand."

After some hesitation, Roger dropped his six-shooter to the grass.

"I deserve some of that money," Roger said.

"You don't deserve shit. It's blood money. Three people died because of it. I'm taking it back where it belongs, and if you try to stop me, I'll kill you. All of you remember that. I'd just as soon kill three of you as one of you. Keep that in mind. Now you go stand over by your friend there. I'll take care of your brother."

The snake hissed. Nick whimpered. Karl looked as if he'd died but had failed to fall over. Roger looked angry.

"I want to see his face in that hole. I hope you won't deprive me of that, Fargo."

"Just get over there with your friend."

But Roger wasn't about to give up. "I meant what I said. I want to see you put his face in that hole."

"Brotherly love. Now move."

As Roger walked around the hole to join his friend Karl, Nick said, "I sure never thought I'd be happy to see you, Fargo." He sounded like a nervous kid.

"You shouldn't be," Fargo said calmly, "because I'm going to put your face in that snake hole myself."

Nick let go with a jumble of nasty names. They had the force of gunshots on the prairie silence.

Fargo walked up to the cover and raised his toe. He nudged the cover about a full inch from the side of the hole. No hissing, no rattling this time around. Just an ominous quiet.

Fargo bent down and grabbed a handful of Nick's hair. He could see blood on the scalp from where Roger had yanked it before.

He started dragging Nick's face to the inch-wide darkness below the edge of the cover.

"You ready, Nick? I'm going to give this another nudge and push your face in."

Fargo had figured it would take a little more than this to have the desired effect on Nick. But Fargo didn't know just how terrified Nick was of snakes.

No man ever skinned alive by Indians had cried out with the horror that Nick managed to pack into his scream—and the scream soon became sobbing.

"I'll tell you! I'll tell you!" Nick sobbed.

"Make it fast."

He made it fast. Fargo had no doubt he was telling the truth.

40

An hour later, Sheriff Cordell came over the rise that looked down on Allie's place. The front door was open. No sign or sound of anybody. He knew something was wrong, bad wrong. He reached down and slid his carbine from its scabbard.

He came loping down the hill. He was prepared for anything. Somebody opening fire on him. A bloody man staggering out the front door. Or a slew of bodies on the floor inside. Houses of death had a different feel, almost an aura of blood. He would never forget the day he'd come upon the farmhouse of a friend. A bone-deep chill had gone through him. He had no physical evidence that anything was amiss. It should have been like any other visit. There would be the kids and the dogs and the cats and the wife in the kitchen. But from his first sight of the house, he'd known better. And a few minutes later, after knocking on the front door and getting no response, he had stepped inside and found everybody dead. He'd gone outside and vomited, and then he'd leaned against the front of the house and wept. His friend had killed them all, and then himself.

He got the same sort of chill now as he dismounted and walked up to the door, passing a large prairie rattler that had been shot several times, chunks of its meaty body being wolfed down by a roaming dog.

Then, inside.

He saw Allie. She was at the stage after death when waxiness had set in on her face and where the final gesture—in this case, her hands held out before her—had a posed look that almost gave it an aspect of being fake. This wasn't really Allie but some kind of life-size doll.

The stench of blood told him otherwise. Flies were having a picnic. Soon enough the maggots would troop forth and invade her body like an army seizing a country.

Small pieces of rope told him that at least one, maybe two, people had been tied up here. He tried to surmise what had happened but, other than knowing that a snake had been shot apart and that Allie had been murdered, guessing was impossible.

He went back outside. He was shiny with cold sweat. He shivered in the cutting autumn wind. He walked the grass to a trail leading east from the house. He got down on his haunches. He counted four different horses, all headed the same way. They probably hadn't counted on anybody following them. But they'd sure made things easy, as long as they stayed on this trail.

He looked back at the house. There was the air of the battlefield about it. He thought of his own war experience. He'd worn blue. But when you saw them all dead on a field, blue or gray didn't matter much. They were just dead folks. Whatever had happened in this house had been conducted with the same kind of fury.

As soon as he got back to town, he'd get the funeral man out here. Then Allie could be buried with the rest of her luckless kin, hardscrabble poor people like so many who had rushed to the frontier to better their lot, but who didn't have the good fortune or scruples or proper work ethic to survive in a savage land.

Poor little Allie. Her life had changed when she took up with Nick Crowley, and she hadn't lived long enough to help it change back to the days when she'd been sweet and clean.

Cordell climbed his horse and set out to follow the tracks on the trail.

Fargo kept his carbine on all three of them: Roger in the lead, Karl in the middle, Nick in the back, closest to Fargo.

Roger knew where they were going. As soon as Nick had said that the money sack was in "Gunsight Tree," Roger said that he should have thought of that. Shortly after, they left Allie's and started out for the tree.

Fargo wanted it done with. He was sick of all of them. He just wanted the money and Nick turned over to Cordell. And then he wanted to ride away. Roger and Karl could handle their fates as they saw fit.

The day darkened. Storm clouds hung heavily in the sky suddenly and the temperature felt as if it had dropped at least five degrees. Fargo had the animal impulse to seek shelter. But there was the damned job to be done.

Then trouble came fast.

Nick, whose wrists were bound, managed to turn his horse around by grabbing the reins with his fingertips and then spurring his horse right toward Fargo.

"Help me, Roger!" Nick cried as he charged.

Roger turned his horse around and charged Fargo too. Fargo's Ovaro shied away from Nick's approaching horse, then, seeing Roger's charging horse, took off at a bolt. Fargo was thrown off balance and fell to the ground. Nick leaped off his horse and threw himself on top of Fargo.

"Hurry!" Nick shouted at his brother.

Roger didn't disappoint him. He dropped from his own horse, ran over to where Nick lay on top of Fargo, pinning him down long enough for Roger to sneak in and kick Fargo so hard on the shoulder that his fingers eased up on the carbine he held. Fargo still tried to keep hold of it but Roger kicked him hard enough in the head to knock him out. The rest was no problem. With Fargo unconscious, Roger had no trouble untying his brother's wrists. And Nick had no problem grabbing Fargo's Colt.

While all this had been going on, all Karl had done was sit his saddle. He seemed dazed.

"You sure were a big help," Nick snapped.

"Leave him alone, Nick. I helped you—that was all that mattered."

"That's right. You did." Then Nick did something

unthinkable—something he'd never done in his entire life—he threw his arms around his brother and hugged him. "You're just like me after all, Roger. And I'm damned glad to see it."

They mounted up and rode. Nick blustered about how things were all coming together. He sounded half-crazed with exuberance, but Karl ended that exuberance. After they'd been riding awhile, Karl said, "You two go on. I'm going back to town."

"My ass you're going back to town," Nick said.

"I can do what I want," Karl said.

"Tell him, brother," Nick said. "He ain't going back to town."

"It doesn't matter what he does," Roger said. "We can't ever go back there, anyway."

"He goes back and tells Cordell and we've got a posse after us."

Roger sighed. "Just ride with us, Karl. We'll get the money and then you can go back."

"All this is crazy, Roger. You don't want to be like Nick. He's a pig, and you've known that all your life. You should come back with me. Let him have the money. They'll be chasing him the rest of his life. You and I aren't cut out for that kind of life." He looked at his friend down the years—all the years back to when they were little boys. Now Karl's family life looked pretty damned good to him. He'd tell Clemmons what he'd done and then arrange to borrow the money and pay Clemmons back. And then he'd take his family—maybe he'd even give up beating his wife—and they'd move to another town and start all over. "C'mon, Roger. Go back to town with me now. Before it gets any worse for us."

Roger looked at Nick.

"You're not going back and you know it, Roger. You're going with me."

"You going to stay here with him?" Karl asked.

Roger began feeling some of Karl's remorse. Maybe going back would be the wise thing. Make his peace with the old man. Ask for forgiveness. Find a different job somewhere else.

"You going to ride with me, Roger?" Karl asked.

Roger sighed. "I guess I can't, Karl. I'm sorry. Give my best to my wife and kid, will you?"

"I sure wish you'd change your mind, Roger."

"Just get the hell out of here, and I mean right now," Nick said.

Karl glanced at Roger and shook his head. He knew what was ahead for his old friend. Death. Everywhere Nick Crowley rode, death rode along. Then Karl spurred his horse and took off fast.

Before he was five yards gone, Nick raised Fargo's Colt and shot him four times in the back.

You could almost hear Roger scream above the roar of the gunfire.

Less than half an hour later, the Crowley brothers moving ahead on the narrow, dusty trail, Sheriff Cordell found Fargo back where the Crowleys had left him.

Fargo was standing, but after the pounding his head had taken over the past few weeks, he was standing none too steadily. In fact, when Cordell appeared, Fargo had a moment when he couldn't even put a name to the somewhat familiar face. Then the name came unbidden. "I figure they're maybe half an hour ahead of us."

"You're bleeding."

Fargo managed a smile. "The way my luck's been running, I'm surprised I've got any blood left."

Cordell climbed down from his horse. He bore a welcome gift. A full flask of rye.

"Now that's something I could use," Fargo said, feeling an open cut on the back of his head. He took two deep swallows, started to hand the flask back, then stopped and took a third swallow.

Cordell wiped the lip of the flask off and took his own drink. "Think we can catch them before nightfall?"

"Maybe. You ever heard of something called 'Gunsight Tree'?"

"Sure. It's where kids used to play all the time."

"They don't anymore?"

Cordell shook his head. "Couple things happened there about ten years ago. One little girl got snatched by somebody and never has turned up. Then a boy fell out of the tree, snapped his neck and died. And then another boy got bitten by a rattler and died before they could even get him to the doc. Parents won't let their kids play on it anymore. And I don't blame 'em. That many deaths—and they happened all in about four, five months of each other—it's just kind of spooky."

"Where is it?"

Cordell shrugged. "Less than an hour if we ride fast."

Fargo was already shoving his boot into the stirrup. "Then let's ride fast."

"You going to explain everything to me sometime, Fargo?"

"Sure," Fargo said, "sometime."

41

The moment he saw Karl Haskins pitch off his horse, Roger Crowley ran to him despite the barked orders of his brother not to do so.

Karl was already dead. There wouldn't be any of those teary last words you found in dime novels and stage plays. There wouldn't even be a memorable and profoundly sad last look from the dying man. There was just blood and the stench of Haskins's bowels and the odd, inscrutable expression of a dead man.

Nonetheless, Roger held his friend's head and shoulders in his arm, unwilling to let either touch the ground. To do so would force him to admit that Karl was really dead, that Nick had killed him without mercy and that Roger's own life had finally overwhelmed him to the point where he knew he'd lost control. Events dictated his behavior and feelings now. He couldn't even pretend to be in charge of his life.

Nick, standing behind him, was shouting, "Leave him alone. We need to get to the tree before dark."

Roger did as he was told. There was something comforting about having somebody else run your life. Tell you to do this or that the way Nick had always wanted to do. You didn't have to think about anything painful. You just followed orders.

Roger lowered his friend's head to the ground. Roger now had blood all over his hands where it had been seeping from Karl's back. But in his daze—which was really a withdrawal from a world totally alien to him now—he no longer felt any loss over Karl. If there were loss to be felt, Nick would tell him to feel it.

Roger stood up and brushed dust from his clothes.

Nick saw his brother's strange expression and said, "Just twenty more minutes, brother, and we're both going to have a lot of money. Our own money. And our old man can't tell us a damned thing about how to spend it. We can ride out from this town and never come back. Now I don't know about you, son, but that makes me feel mighty good."

Roger said nothing. He walked to his horse. Nick saw the blood on his hands.

"You can wash that blood off at the crick over there."

Roger said nothing. Climbed up on his horse. Took the reins. Then Nick realized that Roger was waiting for him to ride lead. Like the old days. Roger always deferring to his brother. Not just the old days but the good old days, when Nick ran everything. Before Roger got bitter and quit listening to anything Nick said.

Nick took his own reins in his hands and led the way toward the waiting tree.

When Fargo saw Karl Haskins on the ground, half lost inside a long, late-afternoon shadow, he said, "Looks like they're having some disagreements."

"That'd be Nick who killed him." On the last part of this journey, Fargo had explained everything to the lawman. Sheriff Cordell did a lot of head shaking. "Old Man Crowley can be a real bastard. But I sure wouldn't wish this on him. Both his sons. He might not have been the best father in the world but he sure deserves better than this. Just hard to fathom Roger throwing in with something like this."

"Or Karl?"

"Especially Karl. Roger had a temper at times. But Karl—" He made a face. "The only person he ever beat up was his wife. But otherwise he was about the most timid man I've ever known."

"Money," Fargo said. "The way Roger told it they both embezzled some from their bosses to invest in this gold mine."

"Gold mine? I'll be damned. Two of the sharpest businessmen in the whole Territory fell for some gold mine?"

"Guess so. At least the way they told it. So when the gold mine didn't work they were stuck with paying it back. Fast. Because in Roger's case, there was going to be an audit. And then the figures looked funny to Clemmons, so Karl was pretty desperate, too."

"Damn," the lawman said. "It just doesn't figure, especially for Roger. He's about the smartest man I've ever known."

Fargo frowned. "Not anymore, he isn't."

42

The Gunsight Tree—so named because when you climbed it you could see almost entirely across the valley below— was on the northwestern tip of the Crowley land, an abnormally massive pine that stretched the equivalent of three stories into the sky, with some branches strong enough to support the weight of two grown men. About three-quarters of the way up the tree was a hollowed-out area big enough to hide even a large canvas bag of money in, which is what Nick had done. Once he'd positioned the bag inside, he'd covered it up by stuffing lengths of pine in front of it. Unless you were standing next to the bag, you wouldn't see it.

The tree was on the edge of a glade dotted with small boulders that made it an ideal place for youngsters to play cowboys and Indians. The fence that enclosed the glade made it even better. Unless you were a kid—Old Man Crowley liked kids just fine—you hesitated to climb the fence and stand on property belonging to the Crowleys. If the old man was in the mood, he might have one of his cowboys chase you off with a shotgun, or even give you a beating. So the glade and the Gunsight Tree were perfect for kids—and the tree perfect for hiding things.

"I should've thought of you hiding it here," Roger Crowley said. He had finally come out of his daze. He doubted that the shock of seeing Karl killed would ever quite leave him. But now Roger had to worry about himself. His escape.

"I figured you'd forget. You and the rest of the town. I just picked the unlikeliest place. And nobody's bothered it."

Roger had already told him about the sense he'd had of somebody following them. Nick had dismissed the notion until now when he said, "You might just be right about somebody being behind us. You take your carbine and crouch behind that boulder over there. I want some cover when I go up in the tree."

Roger had to fight a smile. He was surprised that Nick would give his brother such an advantage. The moment Nick had the moneybag and had reached one of the lower branches, Roger was going to kill him and take all the money for himself. A lot of bitterness, a lot of rage—rage capped by the murder of Karl Haskins—would be put into the bullets that killed Nick.

"Take those horses into the woods while I start climbing, then get to that boulder."

"Yes, sir, Commander, sir."

"What kind of bullshit is this? I thought we buried the hatchet."

In your head is where I'd like to bury it, Roger thought.

"Just get up there and get the money, Nick."

"Now who's playing boss man?"

Roger scowled. "Just get it over with."

He was sicker of Nick than he'd ever been in his entire life. He turned and walked away to grab the reins of the horses and hide them in the woods. He paid no attention to Nick whatsoever.

Both Roger and Nick Crowley were so caught up in their respective tasks that they didn't notice the two men who'd ground-tied their mounts somewhere back down the trail and were now observing them from a shallow stand of trees on the far side of the glen.

Fargo whispered, "We'll wait till Nick jumps down with the money. Then we go after them."

"I'd just as soon shoot him from here."

Fargo smiled. "What about law and order?"

Sheriff Cordell grinned. "I could get away with killing him. You think I couldn't?" He tapped his badge.

"I guess you're right about that, Sheriff."

Dusk was spreading across the sky like a black curtain covered with gleaming pinpoints of stars. You could hear the smallest and saddest sounds of animals making their cries at the end of the day. They were vulnerable to the night and gave it over to creatures more clever and deadly. All they wanted was a place to hide and protect their wee ones.

A cold wind came up and blew the scents of weeds and loam and autumn smoke across the glade. Fargo and Cordell hunkered down in their clothes.

They watched as Roger, after hiding the horses, squatted down behind a boulder. He had just positioned himself when the roar came. Fargo couldn't ever remember a human being making a sound as violent and threatening as this one. He'd read somewhere that Celtic warriors, naked and covered in blood, used to terrify their enemies by making noises that could immobilize their foes.

The rage came from far up in the Gunsight Tree, which Nick had scrambled up with apelike prowess.

The tree was lost in the dusk. They could hear him but not see him. Neither Fargo nor Cordell could figure out what had happened. What could have inspired so much anger?

Roger stood up, a silhouette slightly darker than the dusk. He watched his brother make a noisy descent. He had his gun drawn. He was about ready to shoot when Nick dropped from a branch to the ground and said, "It's gone! Somebody found out about it and took it!"

Not only did Roger not shoot his brother as he'd planned to, he stood there laughing at the news his brother had just brought him.

"What the hell's so funny, smart boy?"

"It's just—it had to end this way. Everything else has gone to hell—why not this, too? The minute I decided to take money from our old man, nothing's gone right. So this shouldn't be any surprise." The somewhat dazed tone was back in Roger's voice.

But his tone only irritated his brother further. "Maybe you figured it out and took it; maybe you only came here so I'd think you didn't have anything to do with it."

"Good old Nick. The craziest bastard west of the Mississippi. Believe me, brother, if I had that money I'd be a long ways from here—a long ways."

"And that's just what you'd say, too. That bullshit about you'd be a long ways from here if you had the money. That's exactly what you'd say. So where the hell is it?"

Roger laughed in disbelief. "Nick, listen to me. I didn't take the money. I didn't have any idea where it was. And like I said, if I had taken it I'd be long gone by now. Somebody else took it, Nick. Somebody else."

Even though Roger still held his carbine, they were in the part of the glade where the night shadows made seeing just about impossible. So by the time he recognized what Nick was doing it was too late.

Nick fired three times, shouting all the time, "You took my money! You took my money!" in the uniquely insane voice that always came to him when he suspected that somebody had betrayed him. Even above the roar of the gunfire, Nick's accusation could be heard in the night. Nobody could ever sound crazier than Nick.

By the time the second shot was fired, Fargo had slipped across the glade, staying to the shadows. When Roger crumpled to the ground, Fargo was within shooting range, standing behind a sweet-smelling pine on the edge of the woods so Nick couldn't see him.

He was about to shout a warning to Nick to drop his weapon when a phantom of shadow, limned by moonlight, stepped out of the woods about ten feet in front of Nick.

Fargo wasn't sure who the tall man was until he spoke.

"You always wanted to kill your brother, Nick. Looks like you finally got the job done."

Crowley. Nick's father. The words came out gentle and sane. Yet beneath them there was a sorrow so deep Fargo couldn't imagine it. He'd never experienced the sorrow of blood before—brother against brother, father against son.

"I'll be honest, Nick. You were always my favorite of you two boys. But I can see now what a mistake it was. You never gave a damn about any of us. You just used the family name to get what you wanted, and to hell with the shame you brought down on us. You always thought you were so damned clever, Nick. But it finally caught up with you, didn't it? That robbery—the *federales* came down on you and you'd never had anybody like them, or this Fargo, on you before. So you end up with no money and killing your own flesh and blood. You're at the end of the line, boy. The end of the line."

Crowley paused and then raised his hand. There was a bag of some kind in it.

"This is what you're looking for. I hired Fargo to follow you. But then I remembered the Gunsight Tree here, and how you boys used to hide things in it. Well, here it is, Nick. Your money. And I even killed your associates for you. Back when I thought I might protect you. I got Sievers first, and then I got Allie. I tried to pin it on Fargo so he wouldn't find out any more about your involvement in the robbery. I even planted evidence for the sheriff to find. You would've killed them yourself and taken their shares, too, because that's how you are. I hate to admit it—but that's how you are and always will be."

He tossed the canvas bag onto the ground between them.

"You son of a bitch," Nick said.

"I want you to drop your gun, Nick. I'm taking you in to Cordell. And whatever happens to you happens. I won't even get an attorney for you. Not after you killed Roger. Now drop the gun, Nick."

Leaving the shelter of the trees, Fargo said, "I've got you covered from behind, Nick. Do what your father says." He walked until he was only five yards from Nick.

"Drop it, Nick," Crowley said. "There's no sense in you dying, too."

Nick laughed bitterly. "You'd kill me, old man? Your own flesh and blood, like you said about Roger? Your own flesh and blood?"

And just as he'd done with Roger, Nick opened fire, getting his father twice in the forehead. Then he pitched himself to the ground and rolled, before Fargo could get off a shot in the gloom.

He fired at Fargo, missing him only by inches. But Fargo stood his ground, knowing that he had just a few seconds to do what he needed to. Even though he couldn't see well in the shadows, he took an educated guess at where Nick was and put three shots in the invisible target.

A cry told him he'd been lucky.

He walked over to the area where he knew Nick lay. He was just about to reach him when the silhouette of Nick's arm came up and squeezed out the last shot in his barrel.

Now it was Fargo's turn to make a wounded-animal sound. Bastard had caught him just on the edge of his shoulder. So it was with great pleasure that Fargo used his own last two shots to rid the world of a spoiled brat who'd used his father's name to get just about anything he wanted. But just now he got something he hadn't wanted, death.

Cordell, who'd been half running, came over to Fargo and said, breathless, "All three of 'em are dead?"

"Sure looks that way, Sheriff."

Cordell laughed bitterly. "Remind me never to invite you back to our little town again."

Fargo's luck took a decided turn for the better. In the confines of her examining room, it was the sumptuous Dr. Rena Adams herself—that angelic face, that devilish body—who repaired the laughably minor shoulder wound Nick Crowley had inflicted on Fargo.

When she was finished, she said, "Your condition isn't as good as you might think."

"Really?"

"No. I think you need a special kind of treatment."

Fargo picked up the playful tone. "But what if I can't afford it?"

"Oh, I'll just give it to you free of charge."

And with that she began unbuttoning her frilly white blouse, revealing the perfectly formed breasts that lay inside.

"Well, ma'am, I sure couldn't refuse that now, could I?"

She guided his large hand to her left breast, then gasped when he began to play with her nipple.

"No, ma'am," he said, "I sure couldn't turn down an offer like this one."

LOOKING FORWARD!

**The following is the opening
section of the next novel in the exciting
Trailsman series from Signet:**

THE TRAILSMAN #300
BACKWOODS BLOODBATH

*The backwoods of Illinois 1860—where treachery
lurked behind every tree and a nation's fate hung
in the balance.*

Skye Fargo was having one of those nights when Lady Luck
sat on his shoulder. He had won two hundred dollars at
poker, bucked the tiger at faro and won sixty-seven dollars
more, and was now back at the poker table with a stack of
chips in the center of the table that promised to add five
hundred to his poke if he won the pot.

The only thing better than a winning streak was a willing
woman, and Fargo's luck had held in that regard, too. A
dove by the name of Saucy had taken a shine to him earlier
that night when he strolled in through the batwings. She
was like a she-bear drawn to honey—and he was the honey.

Miss Saucy McBride was quite an eyeful. Red hair cascaded in curls to bare white shoulders as smooth as alabaster. She had an oval face distinguished by full, upturned lips that appeared as succulent as ripe cherries. A scarlet dress clung to her full figure as if painted on. But it was her eyes that most interested Fargo—hazel pools of desire mixed with a healthy sense of humor.

At the moment, Saucy was perched on Fargo's lap with one arm around his neck and the other resting on his thigh. She was making small circles on his leg with the tips of her fingers. Fargo wanted to throw her to the sawdust-covered floor and have her right there, but there was the matter of winning the five hundred dollars.

Four other players were at the same table. One had already folded. Another was a mousey store clerk who only bet when he had a sure hand, which always turned out to be an especially good one.

The third player, a chunky bank teller partial to cheap, foul-smelling cigars, played like a bull in a china shop. He bet practically every hand, and bluffed as often as he held good cards. There was no predicting him, although Fargo had noticed that the last two times the teller bluffed, he removed his cigar from his mouth and tapped it in the astray before betting.

The fourth player was cut from a whole different cloth. Hale Tilton was a gambler by profession. He favored a black jacket and pants, and frilled white shirts. A wide-brimmed black hat was tilted low over his eyes so no one could read his expression. He, too, was unpredictable, although slightly less so in that he did not bluff as often as the teller. When he did, it was because he sensed weakness in the others' hands.

The teller was about to bet. He took his cigar from his mouth, tapped it on the ashtray, and pushed in fifty dollars.

"Interesting," Hale Tilton said, and added fifty of his own.

It was Fargo's turn. He had two queens, a king, an eight and a three. Only one queen and the three were of the same suit. It was not a great hand but it had potential. He debated discarding the king, eight, and three and asking for three cards, then decided to only discard the eight and the three. But first he had to bet.

Fargo was fairly certain the teller was bluffing. The store clerk had at least a pair of jacks or he would not have opened. Hale Tilton might have a good hand or might be counting on the draw. Either and all ways, Fargo was not about to bow out with a pair of queens. He added fifty dollars and asked for two cards.

The player who had folded was dealing. Another townsman, he wore a brown jacket and bowler, and could never seem to sit still. He was forever fidgeting. Fargo took it to be because the man had a nervous temperament, but now, as the man flicked cards to the store clerk, Fargo saw something that set his blood to boiling. If there was one thing he could not stand, it was a cheat.

Hale Tilton, in the act of stacking his chips, froze for a brief instant with his fingers poised over the table. Then slowly, almost sadly, he lowered his hand and said softly, "Well, well, well."

"What's the mater, Tilton?" the dealer asked with a smirk. "Not getting the cards you need?"

"Oh, I have no complaints," the gambler responded. "Not about the cards, anyway. It's simpletons who get my dander up. They mistakenly think I'm as simpleminded as they are."

"Surely you're not referring to any of us?" the teller demanded, his cigar clenched in a corner of his mouth.

"Not you, no," Hale Tilton said. He focused on Fargo. "Do you want to do this or would you rather I did the honors?"

Fargo had played the gambler a few times before. He did not know Tilton well, but as rumor had it, Tilton was fairly honest, for a cardsharp, and had a reputation as a gent who should not be crossed. "Be my guest," Fargo said, and leaned back.

Hale Tilton glanced from the dealer to the store clerk and back again. "It always amazes me when peckerwoods try."

"Try what?" the clerk nervously asked.

"In case you have forgotten, I gamble for a living. From Mississippi riverboats to prairie hovels to log saloons along the Columbia River, I have seen it all and done it all where cards are involved."

The dealer snickered. "Are you bragging or complaining?"

"I am making a point, Niles," Hale Tilton said. He pushed his chair back and placed his forearms on the table, and if anyone besides Fargo noticed the slight metallic scrape Tilton's right wrist made, they did not show it. "I've seen trimmed cards, cards with sliced corners, cards with bumps. I've seen holdouts of all kinds. Up the sleeve, in vest pockets, in belts. I've seen card cheats use special spectacles to read phosphorescent ink on the backs of cards. I've seen men use bugs."

Fargo had been in a saloon in Kansas when a man was caught using a bug. Made of steel and shaped like a money clip with two sharp ends, the bug was jammed under a table and held cards the bug's owner palmed until they were needed. The man in Kansas had been fortunate. Instead of stretching his neck, as was customary, the other players tarred and feathered him.

Niles glowered at the gambler. "There are a thousand and one ways to cheat, Tilton. What of it?"

"Usually only professionals mark cards and use holdouts," Hale Tilton remarked. "Amateurs deal from the bottom of the desk or play with a friend and set up secret signals, or both." The gambler stared squarely at Niles. "How you two expected to get away with it is beyond me."

"I don't know what you're talking about," Niles huffed. He slid his right hand close to the edge of the table, and to his open brown jacket.

Tilton switched his hard stare to the store clerk. "And you, Weaver. Why would you try it? Don't I always play fair with you boys when I visit Kansas City?"

Weaver paled and looked at Niles, who angrily demanded, "Are you accusing the two of us of cheating? Of working together to fleece a few hands?"

"That is exactly what I am saying, yes," Hale Tilton said.

"But you are free to prove me wrong. Turn over your cards, Mr. Weaver, and show us what Mr. Niles has dealt you."

Fargo patted Saucy on the fanny and bobbed his chin. A veteran of her trade, she understood immediately; she rose and moved well away from the table. Fargo lowered his right hand and hooked his thumb in his belt next to his Colt.

Weaver was not especially brave but he knew his poker. "I am not required to show my hand until the betting is done. That's the rule."

"No one else is going to bet," the gambler said quietly.

"Even so," Weaver said, his voice rising, "I'm not turning my cards over, and that's final."

"You *are* turning them over," Hale Tilton insisted, "or this will be your final day on earth."

Nearby players and patrons had overheard. A current of hushed voices rippled through the room. All eyes turned to their table. The more prudent sidled elsewhere to avoid taking a stray slug.

Fargo happened to notice one man who did not. Another townsman, he sported bushy sideburns and, like Niles, wore a bowler. The man had been idly watching their game. Fargo had not thought anything of it until now. He realized that the man was standing behind Hale Tilton but to one side, where Tilton was less apt to notice.

A conviction came over Fargo that there was more to Niles's and Weaver's shenanigans. On a hunch, he casually shifted in his chair, and sure enough, another townsman was behind him. It set him to wondering why they had let him win so much. Maybe he was imagining things. But then, it was his habit to keep his cards flat on the table and slide them close to the edge before taking a quick peak. The man behind him had not been able to see his cards.

The bank teller removed his cigar and jabbed the lit end at Niles. "Is what he says true? Have you and Weaver been cheating us?"

"Of course not, Sam," Niles said unconvincingly.

"Because if you have," the teller went on, "it stands to reason this isn't the first time."

Niles colored the same shade as a beet and snapped, "I tell you it's not true! Why in hell don't you believe me?"

Sam jabbed the air with his cigar again. "Because it explains how you manage to win so often on days that me and some of the other boys get paid. Or didn't you think any of us would notice?"

"I don't have to sit here and take this!" Niles declared, and started to rise. He stopped when Hale Tilton's right arm rose and extended in his direction, Tilton's fingers bent slightly back.

"You are not going anywhere until your friend turns over the cards you dealt him," the gambler said in a low tone, pregnant with menace.

Weaver was squirming in his chair like a chipmunk on a hot rock. "Niles? What do I do?"

"You don't turn over the cards and you keep your damn mouth shut." Niles gazed expectantly around the room, but if he was hoping for support from any of the onlookers, he was disappointed. No one was willing to intervene. Cheating at cards, like stealing a horse, was a serious offense.

"The cards, Mr. Weaver," Hale Tilton said quietly.

Trembling like an aspen leaf in a brisk breeze, Weaver reached for his cards, but stopped at a sharp cry from Niles.

"Don't you touch them, damn you! He has no right to make you! We will forget about this hand. Everyone can take their money from the pot, and that will be that."

"No, it will not." The gambler slowly rose. "My patience has a limit, gentlemen. I strongly suggest you do as I have asked."

Without being obvious, Fargo was keeping an eye on the townsman behind Tilton and the townsman behind himself. The gambler, preoccupied with Niles and Weaver, had not noticed them.

"You can go to hell!" Niles blustered.

"After you," Hale Tilton said.

"Someone send for the marshal!" Niles clutched at a legal straw. "He'll put a stop to this nonsense."

No one moved. No one offered to go. The bartender brought his hands up from under the bar. He was holding a shotgun but he did not point it at their table. He was content to let the confrontation play itself out without interference unless he absolutely had to step in.

Fargo edged his right hand closer to his Colt. Experience had taught him that when the explosion came, it would be swift and brutal.

Hale Tilton leaned across the table. With his left hand he turned the cards in question over. "Just as I thought."

Four aces and a king lay there for all to see. Too late, Weaver snatched at them and clutched the cards to his chest. "It wasn't my idea," he said.

"Hush, damn you!" Niles fumed. "He can't prove anything if you keep your fool mouth shut!"

"Who needs to?" the gambler asked. "What will it be? Parade you down the street tied to a rail?"

"I would like to see someone try," Niles snarled, and made as if to leave. As he turned, his hand darted under his jacket.

A flick of Hale Tilton's wrist, and just like that a nickel-plated derringer gleamed in the lamplight. The *click* of the hammer was loud enough for Fargo and those at the table to hear. But that did not deter Niles. His arm came out from under his jacket, and so did a Remington.

"Kill the son of a bitch, boys!"

Hale Tilton shot him.

The townsman behind Tilton and the townsman behind Fargo clawed at concealed revolvers. In a heartbeat Fargo was out of his chair with his Colt level. He sent a slug into the man behind the gambler, whirled, and banged off a second shot, all done so fast that, to the onlookers, the two shots sounded as one.

The townsman behind Fargo did not go down. He staggered against the wall, regained his balance, and brought up a Smith and Wesson.

Fargo never did like backshooters. He shot the man in the chest, not once but twice, and at each cracking retort, holes appeared in the townsman's store-bought shirt. The man was dead before his face smacked the floorboards.

Gun smoke hung in the air. Niles was sprawled on his

back with a new hole between his eyes. The townsman behind Tilton was on his side, groaning and mewing about his shoulder being broken.

"I'm obliged for the help," the gambler said.

Fargo scanned the onlookers. None were disposed to avenge the fallen. He started to reload, saying, "There is no shortage of jackasses in this world."

Nodding, Hale Tilton grinned. "If a man can't cheat worth a damn, he should take up knitting."

Now it was Fargo who grinned, but the grin evaporated when what he took to be another townsman came striding purposefully toward them. Quickly, Fargo replaced the last spent cartridge and twirled the Colt so the muzzle pointed at the newcomer. "That's far enough, mister. I have plenty of peas left."

The man stopped. Smiling suavely, he doffed a derby and said with a slight twang, "I assure you, sir, I mean you no harm. Quite the contrary. Your marvelous display has confirmed the reports we have received about you."

"What the hell are you jabbering about?"

"It's quite simple, really." The man's smile widened. "My associates and I would like to hire you to kill someone."

No other series has this much historical action!

THE TRAILSMAN

Available wherever books are sold or at
penguin.com

S310

Penguin Group (USA) Online

What will you be reading tomorrow?

Tom Clancy, Patricia Cornwell, W.E.B. Griffin,
Nora Roberts, William Gibson, Robin Cook,
Brian Jacques, Catherine Coulter, Stephen King,
Dean Koontz, Ken Follett, Clive Cussler,
Eric Jerome Dickey, John Sandford,
Terry McMillan, Sue Monk Kidd, Amy Tan,
John Berendt...

You'll find them all at
penguin.com

*Read excerpts and newsletters,
find tour schedules and reading group guides,
and enter contests.*

Subscribe to Penguin Group (USA) newsletters
and get an exclusive inside look
at exciting new titles and the authors you love
long before everyone else does.

PENGUIN GROUP (USA)
us.penguingroup.com